Chapter One

Thunder, lightning and pigeon poo

"One elephant, two elephants, three elephants, four—"

KRAK-AK-AK-BOOOMMKERASSHH. . .

Jack gulped. The storm was definitely going away now. He was sure of it. Every elephant meant about five miles – by the time you'd said it. So if the lightning flashed and you had time to say two elephants before the thunder crashed, the storm was ten miles away.

He'd only got to two elephants a couple of minutes ago, before the thunder followed the lightning. So . . . it now had to be about fifteen miles away. Maybe more. He let out a quiet sigh of relief. He would never admit it to Lewis – after all he was nearly ten, and Lewis

was only seven – but he was quite nervous of thunderstorms. Jack wondered how people in aeroplanes coped with it. Imagine being up in the sky, right in the middle of thunder and lightning!

There was another flash. "One elephant, two elephants, three elephants, four eleph—"

BOOOOMMMMM. . .

Yes. Definitely going away now. Jack felt better.

Lewis, amazingly, had slept right through the whole thing so far! But Jack was a light sleeper and had been awake since the first rumble.

"Oh do stop heavy breathing and go to sleep!" sighed Lewis from the bottom bunk. "It's just a thunderstorm."

"I'm *not* heavy breathing," snapped Jack. "And I *know* it's just a thunderstorm. It's just keeping me awake – that's all."

"Think of nice things," mumbled his little brother, with a yawn. "That's what Mum always says when we can't get to sleep. Think about . . . Tauronia . . . and having tea in Aunt Thea's garden this afternoon. And cleaning the standing stone and all that. . ."

 2

Jack grinned to himself. Thinking about Tauronia – the underground world they had created and filled with monsters – wasn't always the best idea, late at night. Parts of Tauronia were terrifying, with volcanoes and chasms and earthquakes . . . to say nothing of the Candyfloss Fields of Doom. These places may have begun as drawings, as had the creatures that lived among them, but now they were very real indeed – thanks to some magical Merrion's Mead (a gift from Aunt Thea) and an accidental spillage a few months back. Since Jack and Lewis had unexpectedly brought their drawings of Electrotaur and Slashermite to life, their days had been filled with adventure. And danger. Quite a lot of it. The other monsters that followed (all known as Taurs or Mites) hadn't made things any safer.

Still, it was nice to think back to tea with Aunt Thea that afternoon, and the laughs they had had while cleaning the standing stone at the end of her garden. The stone – a large chunk of serpentine rock – was also the Gateway to Tauronia. Jack and Lewis had

 3

drawn a door into it. With just a tiny drop of magic Merrion's Mead, a route into the land of their Taurs and Mites would appear and their favourite monsters could come up and play.

That afternoon, in the warm sun, Lewis had dropped a bombshell.

"There's poo on the Gateway to Tauronia," he said. He looked solemn. "It's icky."

"Well, that won't do," said Aunt Thea, stopping the garden swing dead with a clop of her purple leather boots and nearly making Jack tumble off into the remains of their tea. "Go into my under-sink cupboard and get the stone cleaning kit," said Aunt Thea. "It's about time the gateway had another rub down."

Lewis went into the kitchen and soon returned with a small square tin containing some lavender oil in little plastic bottles and soft cloths, as well as some rougher flannels and a couple of scrubbing brushes for removing any bird droppings.

Even before it had become the gateway to their magical underground world, Aunt Thea had always loved and respected the standing stone and liked to make the red and grey flecked

serpentine gleam. She and Jack had carried a bucket of hot soapy water up the garden, trying not to splosh it down their legs.

Bees droned drowsily in the honeysuckle and birds cheeped contentedly in the trees as they all set to work and soon removed the offending white and yellow blob from the stone – and a few others down the back. With a kitchen chair to stand on, Jack had rubbed oil into the stone at the top, while Aunt Thea and Lewis worked lower down. A lovely smell of lavender wafted around them.

"I always think," said Lewis "that this is a beacon for aliens. They say that about Stonehenge, don't they?"

"They do," agreed his aunt. "And the pyramids. And Avebury Ring. The Aztec temples. The new car park at Asco's. . ." She grinned. "Well, maybe not the new car park at Asco's. Although some of the creatures in it *look* like aliens."

"They said on the news that there were UFOs over Stonehenge the other night," said Jack. "Lights in the sky and all that. Loads of UFO nuts have been camping out there."

"Probably just a publicity stunt," said Aunt Thea. "To get plenty of people through the gift shop!" Then the doorbell rang, so she went to answer it and was engaged in conversation with a salesman when Jack went back to the kitchen in search of more lavender oil. After a bit of rummaging he finally found another little plastic bottle of oil, so went back up the garden and climbed up on the chair again.

"Done!" said Lewis, when Aunt Thea came back, having seen off the salesman. "No poo. All gleamy. Smells nice."

"It certainly does smell nice," agreed Aunt Thea, regarding the gleaming column of rock approvingly. "Good heavens, did you really use up *all* my lavender oil? Two whole bottles?!"

"Three, actually," admitted Jack. "But the first two were only half full anyway. And the last lot wasn't that good. It was a bit runny."

"Funny, I thought I only had two," said Aunt Thea, patting the stone fondly. "Anyway, it looks lovely. No bird will *dare* to drop anything on it again. Even passing beetles would think twice about widdling on it. . ."

Smiling as he thought back to this, Jack had almost drifted off to sleep again when there was a bright flash which made him jump and clutch at his bedclothes. He took a deep breath and willed himself to not be scared as the thunder rumbled some miles away.

All quiet again. Back to sleep.

Tap. Tap-tap.

Jack swung his head down and stared at the dim shape of his little brother under the covers below. "Is that you, Lew?" he whispered.

 7

Lewis's head emerged. "You what?" he mumbled.

"Was that you tapping?" asked Jack.

"What?!"

"Oh forget it – go back to sleep!" Jack pulled himself up and lay back on his pillow.

Tap. Tap tap tap. Phwomp! Phwomp! Phwomp!

Jack shot up in bed again. So did Lewis. "What's that?" hissed Lewis.

Jack stared at the window as another flash illuminated a dark moving shape.

"There's something outside!" he gasped. "And it wants to get in. . ."

Chapter Two

Twenty Minutes Earlier

"Blaagggadag!" said Aunt Thea. Loudly. To nobody in particular. She found herself upside down on top of her quilt, her heart racing and her hair in her face.

Taking a shaky breath, she realized that she had been woken up by the thunderstorm. That huge bang must have been a clap right above the roof. The rain was hitting the window so hard it sounded like a very large audience were applauding the lightning show.

Aunt Thea feared for the glass. Beyond it she could see the sky – its clouds hanging low like a dirty duvet – flickering with many thousands of volts of lightning.

She put herself round the right way and lay

back on her pillows with a smile. Electrotaur would *love* this. She liked thunderstorms herself. She found them very entertaining and exciting – and had seen some whoppers on her many journeys around the world. This was nothing, really. She snuggled back down to enjoy the rest of it, but was soon drifting back to sleep again, lulled by the applauding rain.

Tap tap.

Tap tap tap.

Bang. Bang bang bang.

Aunt Thea sat up again, suddenly, her eyes springing open. The storm was still rumbling around the valley, but *that* wasn't rain. Or thunder.

Bang bang bang bang BANG.

Someone was at the back door. She threw on her green silk dressing gown and ran down the stairs, her red hair flying out behind her. The back door, which led off the kitchen, was made up of several panes of glass. As the lightning flared, she could make out two familiar silhouettes peering through them.

"Electrotaur! Slashermite!" squawked Aunt Thea, in shock and annoyance, unbolting

 10

the door. She threw it open and a shower of raindrops blew into her face.

Electrotaur stood at an impressive eight feet tall, his green eyes crackling as if he'd been charged up by the storm. Which he almost certainly had. His golden scaly body buzzed with pent-up energy and more sparks were pouring off his lightning-shaped fingertips and tail. Aunt Thea wished, for the fiftieth time, that Jack had drawn a less dangerous Taur. Of course, to be fair, her nephew had not been expecting Electrotaur to come to life when he'd first drawn him.

Looking more closely, Aunt Thea saw that the Taur looked worried. But Electrotaur always looked worried. What was more worrying was that *Slashermite* looked worried. In which case, thought Aunt Thea, there probably *was* something to worry about.

Lewis's come-to-life drawing was small and purple with a rhino horn on his nose and metallic blade-like fingers which he was now scraping together anxiously, making a noise like a chef sharpening his knives.

11

"What on earth are you two doing up out of Tauronia, on a night like this?" Aunt Thea demanded. "Do you know what time it is?!"

Slashermite bounced up and down on his scaly purple legs, and accidentally scored some grooves on Aunt Thea's patio with his toe-blades. "But Lady Thea, we were *called*! The masters have called us all, have they not? We think it must be for an epic quest!"

"What?" Aunt Thea screwed up her face and rubbed her tired eyes. "Jack and Lewis aren't even here! Nobody's had the magic mead out. You're just . . . wait a minute. Did you say *all*?"

The Taurs nodded. Aunt Thea pulled them into the kitchen, out of the doorway and then stared out into the storm-swept garden. Her eyes stretched wide and her mouth fell open. A small squeak of dismay escaped from it.

As the sky burst into brilliant white light, her garden revealed the terrifying truth. It was absolutely stuffed with monsters.

A huge, jostling, excited crowd of monsters; all drawn by Jack and Lewis for fun – and then brought to life with magic mead for *more*

fun ... but who were always, ALWAYS kept safely away from the real world in the underground land of Tauronia. Until now.

With every flash more of them appeared, pouring down the garden from the gaping golden gateway in the standing stone. Flowertaur, Slashertaur, Tundrataur, Dragotaur and a whole flock of Dragomites, roosting on the branches of the rowan tree; Ninjataur, leaping silently up on to the greenhouse roof, his navy blue body as sure as a gymnast and his face covered in a navy-blue bandage-like mask beneath his sinister silver eyes; Lavataur, settling on the rockery and turning the nice Welsh cobbles to magma ... and more and more and more...

Her garden was a carnival of multicoloured, multi-limbed, heavily-clawed, thoroughly-scaled and jaggedly-toothed creatures of varying degrees of dangerousness. This one could set fire to things with a hard stare. That one could spit hot treacle. This one could inflict a plague of verrucas and, if memory served her right, that one over *there* could turn anything – and anyone – into fudge.

 13

"Oh – my – word," Aunt Thea gasped, feeling rather faint. She slumped on to the back step. She needed Jack and Lewis. And she needed them NOW.

Chapter Three

Night Flight

Jack felt his heartbeat get faster. The tapping went on. It was definitely on the window. Something was out there, beyond the curtains. Tapping for attention. And phwomping.

"C-could it be a tree branch or something?" squeaked Lewis.

"The nearest tree is at the end of the garden," Jack squeaked back.

There was a sudden, brighter flash of lightning and in an instant Jack and Lewis saw the shape of something large, with wings, hovering outside their window. Jack jumped out of his bunk and Lewis climbed out of his. Fearfully they edged towards their window and took a hold of the curtains. They looked at

15

each other; wide, scared eyes lit up by another flash of lightning.

"One . . . two. . ." said Jack, trying to stop his voice wobbling. "THREE!"

They both whipped open a curtain and stared out into the night. Something *was* hovering beyond the glass. Four eyes stared in at them. Many scales glinted in the light of the storm. Claws flexed. Leathery wings phwomped up and down. A voice called to them through the booming thunder. . .

"Please open up! My blades are going to *rust!*"

"Slashermite!" gasped Lewis, throwing open the window. "What on earth. . .?"

Jack gaped. "Dragotaur! How – what – where?"

Slashermite was *riding* on the neck of Jack's dragon Taur. Dragotaur was emerald green and glistening with jewel-like scales. Her four almond-shaped eyes were the colour of rubies and her long tail had an artistic arrow-head flare on the end. Her claws were curved, sharp and golden, her bat-like wings were fifteen feet

across, and she was capable of breathing out huge jets of flame. She had *never* been outside Tauronia before. How had this happened?

"Master Lewis! Master Jack!" beseeched Slashermite, who was holding on to Dragotaur with some difficulty, as his sharp finger-blades had to be tucked carefully away into his palms. "You must come to Lady Thea at once! Oh! It is an emergency! An emergency!"

"What's happened?" Lewis leaned out of the window into the rain and stared at his creation.

"There are Taurs and Mites everywhere in Lady Thea's garden! They have come out for the quest! They have left Tauronia!"

"WHAT?" squawked Jack.

"Shhhh!" said Lewis. "You'll wake Mum and Dad."

"Please, masters, please!" begged Slashermite. "You must come with us right away! There is no time to lose. You are needed for emergency meading – now – before it is too late!"

"Tell Aunt Thea we're coming," said Jack, throwing his socks and trainers on. "We'll run

 17

through the woods as fast as we can."

"But Master Jack – she was quite insistent that we bring you back NOW!" Slashermite glanced back behind him, along the length of Dragotaur's magnificent body.

"You mean . . . you mean . . . *fly?*" Jack stood up and stared at their proposed transport as it hovered up and down.

"Cool!" said Lewis. His trainers were already on and he was at the open window, putting one foot over the sill.

"Lewis! Stop! Wait!" cried Jack. "That's – that's *so* dangerous. We can't go flying around in the middle of a thunderstorm on a dragon!"

"Yes we can," said Lewis. "You drew her safe for riding, didn't you?"

Jack blinked. Well . . . yes . . . he *had* made Dragotaur the kind of dragon you could ride. She was one of Jack's earliest drawings, made even before they had accidentally discovered that Merrion's Mead was magical and could bring their drawings to life. He had always imagined himself swooping through the sky on Dragotaur's back. He'd even made special

dents along her spiky spine, suitable for up to three riders to settle into, while holding on to the spikes in front. Just as Slashermite was doing now.

Lewis wasn't waiting for an answer. Before Jack could stay "But", he had leaped across on to Dragotaur's back and into the second dent behind Slashermite. He sat astride her easily and then beckoned to Jack to join them. There was nothing else for it. Lewis was going and Jack had to be there to protect his brother – so he was going too. He put his feet out over the sill and tried not to look at the drop to the garden below, lit up by a million raindrops reflecting the lightning.

Helpfully, Dragotaur hovered closer and Jack was able to reach out and grab the spiky ridge of her spine. It was warm and leathery and very, very real. He felt a surge of pride. Dragotaur was fabulous – and she was one of *his* creations. He sprang forward and swung one leg across. He slid comfortably into the third rider's dent and grasped the spine in front. Lewis twisted round to grin at him, his eyes round with excitement.

"This is so *cool!*" he cried.

"Yeah, it is!" croaked back Jack. Then his breath was blown out of him as Dragotaur soared up into the storm.

Chapter Four

Pudding Panic

SPLAT! SPLAT-SPLAT!

"Oh! That is disgusting!" Aunt Thea shuddered.

Three Jellymites had flung themselves at the kitchen window and were now stuck to it, smiling sweetly at her through the glass while sliding down it ever so slowly. She stepped across and rapped hard on the pane. "STOP making a mess of my windows you revolting, sticky little things!"

The Jellymites were about the size of dinner plates, red, wobbly and see-through. They continued to smile and slide, leaving a trail of smeared raindrops and goo in their wake.

Aunt Thea opened the door a crack and

called out, "Blomonjataur! Please collect your Jellymites from off my window!"

There was a gloopy whomping noise as a six foot high orange blancmange trundled down the garden, reached out his wiggly arms and began to peel the offending Mites off the glass, with small squelches. They all began to squeak and shake violently in protest, as Blomonjataur (Lewis had spelled it like it sounded) put them down in a row on the wooden garden bench.

"Hush!" hissed Aunt Thea, eyeing the neighbours' back windows nervously. "Behave yourselves! I won't accept tantrums in my garden – especially not from desserts!"

"They're a bit sensitive," apologized Blomonjataur, as the Jellymites settled down to sniffling and pouting.

"Oh nonsense," muttered Aunt Thea. "They'll be all right in a trifle."

She giggled rather hysterically at her own joke, then shook her head. She was really going to have to have a word with Jack and Lewis about some of their creations. The rain was easing off now, although the occasional flash and rumble told her the storm wasn't quite finished yet. The garden was even more packed with monsters than the last time she'd looked. What if one of her neighbours happened to look down into her garden from an upstairs window? It was quite secluded, but some parts of the lawn could be seen – and they were heaving with horrific beasts. How would she ever begin to explain this? Even now, Flowertaur was trying to climb up the privet hedge and peer over it, his green leafy limbs curling around the bush like creepers and his wide-eyed, smiley face with its pretty fringe of petals disguising the fact that he was a deadly assassin.

"Questy! Questy!" gurgled a familiar voice. "Must chase guff!" Stinkermite, wearing blue knitted hotpants and matching glittery leg warmers, was trying to squeeze past her into the kitchen, his four eyes gyrating wildly with excitement on the ends of their stalks.

"Oh no you don't!" Aunt Thea tried to push the door shut but the Mite was through already and making for the sofa and the TV remote control. Stinkermite had spent some

 23

time in Aunt Thea's house shortly after he was accidentally created and was rather taken with reality TV shows. Electrotraur sat stiffly at the table, his sparking tail scooped up in his flickering hands to avoid damage to the floor. He glared balefully at the Mite as it flicked from channel to channel before settling on an animated Barbie adventure with a gurgle of happiness. For a guff-chasing monster, he had delicate tastes in entertainment. Stinkermite lived on guffergy. If anyone let a really good fart go, he would chase them and surround them in a giant bubble and collect the gas. It wasn't a pleasant thing.

Outside there was a whoosh and a blaze of light. Not lightning this time. "Oh no!" wailed Aunt Thea. "Not my azalea!" Lavataur had just incinerated her favourite shrub. And now Vortexamite, a small spinning tornado of a creature with a tendency to topple over a lot, was whipping the flames up into a cone. "Oh, Jack, Lewis! Where are you?"

"WHOOOOOOOOOO-HOOOOOOOO!"

screamed Lewis as Dragotaur soared in and out of the cold wet storm clouds. Jack just screamed. Fortunately his scream was whipped away from his mouth as soon as it got out, and was lost far behind him. Nobody heard. He gripped on to his creation's leathery spines for dear life, digging his knees and his ankles tightly into the dragon's scaly flanks and hoping this wasn't going to be the end of him. Had he drawn Dragotaur with the ability to loop the loop? He really hoped not.

Up in front of Lewis, Slashermite turned his head around to check on his masters and looked pretty terrified too, Jack thought. Only Lewis was whooping. But then, he liked rollercoasters. Jack hated them. He looked down and saw the wood blur past beneath his feet, lit up by lightning flashes. Wisps of grey cloud were scattered below them, and the occasional swipe of cold wet air on his face told him they were flying *through* some of them. At least the storm was easing off now. He couldn't hear any thunder and the flashes seemed to be further away.

"This is amaaazing!" cried Lewis, as Dragotaur swooped left and right, her warm body undulating like an eel through the cold night air. She seemed to be taking her time, enjoying the dramatic flight. In between the lightning flashes, Jack saw that she was blowing out a series of small balls of fire which were lighting the way ahead of her. In spite of his terror, Jack marvelled at his creation. She was one of his most beautiful Taurs, with delicately-drawn scales, graceful wings and elegant curls of dragon hair under her chin. She'd taken him well over an hour to draw.

Then a burst of hot white light tore past his ear with a deafening crack! Oh no! Had the lightning hit them? Dragotaur shuddered and suddenly tipped steeply forward, nose down, and began to plummet. They all screamed this time, even Lewis. Jack caught a glimpse of the roof of Aunt Thea's house hurtling towards him while his knees shot up behind his head and his hands were whipped away from the spike they'd been clinging to. Dragotaur pulled up from her nosedive, and Lewis and Slashermite tried in vain to grab Jack as he plunged past them, but he was heavier than they were and they couldn't stop him. He was falling too fast to scream now, flipping up and over and down past his own feet with a garden full of stunned Taurs and Mites now staring up at him. He guessed this was his end – his Dragotaur had done for him.

A second later it was all over.

Schoofloowump was the noise Jack made as he landed. . .

Chapter Five

Desserted

. . .in Blomonjataur.

Jack opened his eyes, expecting to see his limbs scattered all over Aunt Thea's lawn, but instead found himself wallowing in a mound of orange goo. Nearby, three hysterical Jellymites were crying, "Blonjy! Blonjy! Wake up, Blonjy!"

"Oops. That's done for Blomonjataur!" said a voice at his ear. Lewis took hold of Jack's sticky, gloopy orange arm and pulled him up out of the mess. "It's all right!" he assured the Jellymites, which were now running to him and trying to climb up his legs. "I'll draw Blonjy OK again – just give me a few minutes." The crying subsided, thankfully. Behind Lewis, Jack could see Dragotaur settling on the roof of the shed, which creaked rather worryingly under her weight.

He looked around at all the other Taurs and Mites and groaned in horror. Slashermite had not been kidding! There were *hundreds* of them here! He could feel the heat from Lavataur as the glowing dripping creature turned the rockery molten and set some pretty Alpine plants smouldering. He could see dozens of Dragomites squabbling in the branches of the rowan tree, hear Vortexamite whipping her tail around and catching some of the jewel-like winged Aviamites in the cyclone. Slashertaur, Tundrataur, Flowertaur, Ninjataur . . . and more, more, more. How could this have happened?! Jack groaned in horror as he and Lewis pushed through the crowd to reach the kitchen door.

Aunt Thea pulled them into the house, Slashermite holding back any creatures who tried to follow with a swift fanning of his finger-blades. "Quick!" she shrieked, not even bothering to check Jack, but thrusting crayons and paper at them. "Get them out of my garden before the neighbours see!"

 29

Jack seized the paper with trembling hands and ran with it to the dining table. With great speed he scribbled a basic square creature with twiggy arms and legs and a rather long-suffering expression and wrote "Sortitoutataur" next to it. Then he added "Gets all Taurs out of garden and back down into Tauronia immediately."

Aunt Thea threw Merrion's Mead across the drawing from one of the little twiggy bottles and a few seconds later there was a gust of wind and Sortitoutataur stood, hands on hips, in the kitchen.

"Oh, so *now* I'm allowed into the house, am I? After waiting out there by your very messy compost heap for I don't know *how* long! I suppose you *want* something again, do you?" he huffed.

"Yes!" shouted Jack, Lewis and Aunt Thea all at once.

"I thought so." Sortitoutataur tutted and cast his hastily scribbled eyes upwards. "Sorting out a *mess* again, is it?"

"Yes!" shouted Jack, Lewis and Aunt Thea.

Aunt Thea took hold of Sortitoutaur's papery shoulders and turned him to face the garden. "You know what to do – Jack wrote it when he meaded you! Please get on with it!"

"All right!" sighed Sortitoutataur. He stepped, rather theatrically, out into the garden and then lifted his hurriedly sketched arms up, like the conductor of an orchestra. "EVERYONE!" he called, in a surprisingly commanding voice. All eyes turned to him and then he waved his arms majestically downwards and in an instant the unwelcome visitors began to swirl around and around, like ants in water going down a plughole.

31

Within five seconds every Taur and Mite had been caught up in the whirlpool and sucked right back down through the standing stone opening. The Dragomites were last to go, as they held on to the tree with tight talons for as long as possible – but finally they too flipped down into the swirling funnel and, with a chorus of annoyed squeaks, were gone.

Silence filled the garden. Apart from a molten rockery and a gently smoking azalea bush, you might never know the monsters had been there.

Sortitoutataur walked back into the kitchen with a rustling, papery sort of sound. He looked very 2D.

"Don't you think you ought to improve him a bit?" asked Lewis, squinting up at the worst drawn Taur they knew. "At least make him three dimensional. You can't see him when he turns sideways."

Sortitoutataur raised a hopeful eyebrow at Jack.

"Sorry," said Jack. "But I've only ever drawn him in an emergency. I've always had to do it

32

really fast. Last time we were surrounded by frozen kids in a finger-knitting swamp and the police were coming, remember? And this time every Taur in Tauronia was bursting into the real world. There's never any time for twiddly bits!"

"Oh, don't worry about *me*. . ." Sortitoutataur sighed, bravely,

"Look, I'll try to make you better looking when I get a chance, but for now, can you just go back to Tauronia too?"

Sortitoutataur sighed again. Then there was a *pop* and he was gone.

Aunt Thea sagged into a chair and dropped her head on to the kitchen table, pulling her arms in tight around it. "We've still got to send these three back," she mumbled through her sleeves, flapping a weary hand in the direction of Electrotaur, Slashermite and Stinkermite, who was still engrossed in the TV.

"But what on earth started this in the first place?" She sat up and looked hard at Jack and Lewis. "That's what *I* want to know! How did the Gateway to Tauronia suddenly open up all of its own accord and start spewing Taurs and Mites out into the Overworld?!"

"It wasn't us!" protested Jack, sitting down between his aunt and Electrotaur and pushing a clump of sticky orange hair out of his eye. He was exhausted. Nobody seemed to have remembered that he'd plummeted to almost certain death about eight minutes ago. "How can you think we'd do something like that?"

"I don't think it. Not really," admitted Aunt Thea. "But something has changed. Something has happened. What, though? And was it something *we* did?"

Lewis sat down too, next to a rather tired-looking Slashermite. He pulled some paper towards him and quickly sketched poor Blomonjataur coming back to life down in Tauronia, surrounded by cheering Jellymites. He'd saved Jack's life, after all! He deserved a bit of fuss. Lewis tipped some mead on to the picture and then put the cork back in.

"Oh do mead Stinkermite back home too, will you?" sighed Aunt Thea. "With the state we're in one of us is bound to let a guff out any

time soon, and he'll start chasing us."

Lewis reached into the kitchen table drawer, pulled out the folder where all the drawings of the Taurs and Mites were kept, found the picture of Stinkermite and quickly wrote "Back home" next to it. Aunt Thea lost no time in meading it. Stinkermite popped out of sight and the remote control dropped on to the sofa with a small thud. Aunt Thea reached over and switched off the TV with a sigh of relief.

"Electrotaur, Slashermite," said Aunt Thea, more calmly now. "Tell me exactly what happened to make you all come up to the Overworld."

Slashermite and Electrotaur sat up straight. "MASTERS CALL," said Electrotaur. "WE COME."

"Ah, Electrotaur. Master of detail," muttered Aunt Thea.

"When the masters call, we feel a tingling," explained Slashermite. "Here," he tapped his forehead, just below the rhino horn. "This is how we know we have a quest. But this time . . . *everyone* tingled! Everyone! We ran to the steps to the Overworld as we always do, and

 35

found a crowd. All said they tingled – that they were called for a quest! Even Grippakillataur! But he could not get up the stairs. He blocked the way – or still more would have arrived. We thought you needed us all to fight a war!" Slashermite's eyes gleamed with excitement at this idea. Lewis remembered that, as fun and friendly as Slashermite was, he *had* been drawn as a warrior.

"So what made everyone tingle?" said Aunt Thea. "What was *different*? There must be something. . ."

"The lightning!" shouted Lewis, jumping up from his seat. "It must have been the lightning!"

Aunt Thea and Jack exchanged glances. "Yes," said Jack. "Yes, it must be that!"

Aunt Thea screwed up her face and rubbed it with tired, worried fingers. "Hmm, a lightning strike on the stone. That must be it, I suppose. How very worrying."

"Look, I think we need to get these two back home, too," said Jack, trying to be sensible.

"Agreed," sighed Aunt Thea. "We all need

to get some sleep. I'm meant to be picking you up at ten, for the Farmer's Market Fair, remember?"

They walked Electrotaur and Slashermite up the garden, to see them back down to Tauronia. "Thank goodness it's all over now, anyway," said Aunt Thea, "and none of my neighbours noticed anything unusual."

"We'd just get Slashermite round to hypnotize them all," said Lewis. He was very proud of the hypnotism power he'd given to his best Mite – and it had certainly helped them out of a few tricky situations.

"Yes, but all the screaming before he gets them done is so wearing," sighed Aunt Thea. Then she stopped dead in her tracks and stared up the garden towards the standing stone. Her eyes widened and her mouth fell open.

The dark stormy sky was calmer – but now it was split in two by a pure beam of blue light, shining straight up, up and up into space.

The beam was coming from the top of the standing stone.

37

Chapter Six

Mite Be Trouble

They all edged up the garden, staring at the blue beam. Its perfectly vertical shaft plunged ever upwards, cutting like a laser through the stormy clouds which scudded across its path.

"What *is* it?" whispered Lewis.

"I don't know. But I didn't think this night could *get* any more worrying," muttered Aunt Thea.

Jack ran into the house for a kitchen chair. Back at the standing stone, he set it down and Aunt Thea, who was the tallest, leaped up on to it, so she could look at the top of the giant finger of rock.

"What can you see?" hissed Jack. "Where's the light coming from?"

"I don't know . . . it seems to be just shining out from inside the rock . . . there's no torch stuck up here or anything like that."

"Let me see!" Jack jumped up on to the chair as soon as his aunt stepped off it. The stone was still wet, although the rain had stopped now and the storm had rolled away to the east, leaving the night air fresh and filled with the smell of soaked leaves, bark and grass. Now Lewis scrambled up beside him, pushing his head under Jack's arm.

They could see their aunt was right. The light was shining out of the stone all right – the speckled serpentine rock was glowing an intense blue, as if lit from inside. Jack put out his hand and the blue beam shone into it and . . . *through* it. His skin let the light pass through and he thought he could see his skeleton bones showing up in it. Lewis put his hand into the beam too. It felt neither warm nor cold, but whatever they did, the beam kept beaming on up into space.

"Boys, do stop doing that," said Aunt Thea. "It could be dangerous."

39

"What, like, radioactive or something?" marvelled Lewis, turning his hand around in the light and looking for his bones, like Jack. "Cool!"

"Come on! Get down now," snapped Aunt Thea. "If your fingers shrivel up and drop off, it'll be *me* who has to answer to your mum and dad! Oh dear, oh dear, oh dear. What ever is happening here, I don't like it at all!"

"Electrotaur, Slashermite, what do you know about this?" asked Jack as he and Lewis

jumped back down on to the soggy grass, which squeaked under their trainers. The Taur and Mite looked at each other, then back at Jack, and shrugged.

"Should we make enquiries in Tauronia for you, masters?" asked Slashermite.

"Yes," said Aunt Thea. "But you'll have to report back to us in the morning. I've had quite enough of the inhabitants of Tauronia for one night. Off you both go now." She briskly sent them down through the gateway and then turned to her nephews. "Come on, I've got to get you two back home and into bed without waking your parents. How on earth would I explain why I've had you two over my place until three a.m., in the middle of a storm?"

They trooped back down the garden, through the house and out to Aunt Thea's black VW Beetle. She hadn't even given them any hot chocolate. That was unheard of! She was very shaken up, Jack could tell. She kept glancing back at the blue beam which rose high above the roof of her cottage and could be seen,

surely, for miles around.

"It'll be all right, Aunty, don't worry!" he said.

She smiled wanly back at him, turning her key in the ignition. "I hope you're right, Jack – but I have no way of knowing whether any of my neighbours looked out and saw my garden full of Taurs. You *can* see into parts of it from my neighbours' bedrooms. All it would have taken was for someone to glance outside to watch the storm – and. . ." She shook her head and huffed out a shaky breath.

"Well, if someone *did* see something, surely a bunch of police cars would have shown up by now," reasoned Lewis.

"Or else they'd have thought they were dreaming," said Jack. "We can talk about it when we go out with you in the morning. And at least we managed to get all the Taurs out of your garden and safely back down to Tauronia."

"Yes," sighed Aunt Thea. "We did at least manage to get rid of the monster party. Thank goodness. Taurs and Mites on the loose in the

42

Overworld. Really, it makes me shudder to think of it. I do hope that beam of light fades soon, though, before everyone wakes up for their breakfast."

She turned left into the road that led around the outskirts of the wood and drove on to where Jack and Lewis lived. The shiny black car trundled along the road, its wheels splashing through fast running floodwater making its way down to the river.

And ambling along the river's banks, trailing tendrils and waving leafy hands with his fascinated round face turned up to the stars, was Flowertaur.

Chapter Seven

Taur on Tour

The first thing Jack did when he woke up the next morning was run to the window and stare out into the sky above the woods. He squinted hard and then put on his spectacles and squinted harder – but he could not see any blue beam shooting up into the heavens. He heaved a sigh of relief.

"Lewis!" he called. "Get up! Aunt Thea should be here soon, to take us to the Farmer's Market Fair."

Lewis burbled from his nest of bedclothes. He tended to burrow into them like a gerbil. Jack located his brother's ear and gave it a tug. "Come on! Get up! It's nearly half past nine!"

One of Lewis's eyes peered out through a gap in his duvet. "I only just fell asleep!"

They hadn't had much sleep, it was true. At just after three in the morning they had crept in through the front door, having used the spare key which their mum hid in the garden, and then tiptoed up the stairs and back to bed. But they'd lain whispering to each other about the night's events for at least another hour.

Now Lewis was paying for it. He lifted his head, groggily, and put one foot out. "Bleeurgh," he commented.

"Wake up, you two sleepy heads!" Mum put her head around the door. "Come on down. I'm doing bacon butties."

Jack and Lewis were at the breakfast table ten minutes later, feeling much revived as they munched crispy bacon sandwiches and drank warm tea.

"Is Aunt Thea coming soon?" asked Jack, reaching for more ketchup.

"Yes, any minute. Honestly, I think you spend more time with Aunt Thea than you do with me," said their mum, fiddling with the radio and trying to get a weather report.

 45

"Maybe she should just adopt you!"

"We love you too, Mum," grinned Lewis. "It's just that the Gateway To Tauronia is in Aunt Thea's garden. . ."

"Yes, yes," muttered Mum, alighting on a local BBC station and tweaking the aerial. "Don't know why you can't organize a Gateway to Taurolia in your *own* garden once in a while. . ."

"Taur-*on*-ia," corrected Lewis. "And we would, but you haven't got a standing stone . . . and you wouldn't want a garden full of Taurs and Mites in the middle of the night, would you?"

"And Aunt Thea *would*?"

"Oh, she didn't mind *that* much," said Lewis.

"You two just *live* in a world of make-believe, don't you?" smiled Mum, as the presenter relayed news about last night's storm and the flooding it had caused.

Jack and Lewis grinned at each other, but they were both worried. They wanted to find out what was happening back at the standing stone.

"...and several roads were still flooded this morning," concluded the radio presenter. "Listen out for our traffic and travel report, in five minutes, for details of diversions. *But* it wasn't just thunder and lightning in our skies last night, according to one listener." The presenter chuckled and added, theatrically: "Apparently *there be dragons!*"

Jack and Lewis froze, mid-munch, and stared at each other in horror.

"Keen-eyed Vera Lambton from Wellshall swears blind that she saw a dragon flying through the storm, right over her house last night. She even took a photo – and we've put it up on the website in case you want to take a look." The presenter chuckled warmly, again. "It's a bit blurry and, OK, it *could* be a goose. But Vera says not ... and (*chuckle, chuckle*) who are *we* to doubt her? Check it out on www dot—"

"Dragon, indeed," said Mum, snapping the radio off and glancing through the window. "Oh, that looks like Aunt Thea's car now. Jack? Lewis? You look like you've seen a ghost!"

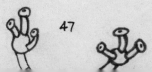

Jack and Lewis coughed and smiled and Lewis put the ketchup away (which only served to bewilder his mother further). "I suppose you two think it was a *real* dragon," she smiled, as they headed out to meet Aunt Thea.

"We've got to get online and have a look at that picture!" Jack hissed to Lewis as they clambered into the back seat of the Beetle while Mum and Aunt Thea had a quick chat.

"What about that storm?" Mum was saying. "Did you hear the radio this morning? Some old dear thought she'd seen a dragon flying through it!"

"No – really?! Well . . . honestly. . ." coughed Aunt Thea. "What some people will say to get on air these days!"

She got in and hurriedly drove off, while Jack and Lewis sat in the back and didn't say anything. After a while she sighed and said, "Can't see the light this morning, but in daylight I can't be sure whether it's gone. I hope it is. Yes. It *is*. It *is* gone – I've decided. So we can all stop worrying and have a nice time at the Farmer's Market Fair. Have you

got pocket money to spend?"

"Yes," said Jack, "and Mum gave us some money for some free range pork sausages."

Twenty minutes later they arrived at a large tree-lined recreation ground on the edge of town with many stalls and little tents where local farmers were selling meat and fruit and vegetables and other fresh produce. Jack and Lewis didn't pay much attention to these, even though the hog roast smelled wonderful. They were more interested in the fairground rides.

Aunt Thea stepped up to a stall selling bread and cheese and started chatting with a woman there. "Boys," she said. "This is my friend, Carol. Carol, this is Jack and Lewis – my nephews."

"Oh, I've heard all about you!" smiled Carol, who wore jeans, wellies and a green jacket and her dark hair tucked under a peaked cap. She looked friendly but rather tired.

"Carol is a farmer, remember? With her husband, Neil," Aunt Thea told Jack and Lewis. "She grows crops and keeps dairy cows further up county."

49

"Oh yes," remembered Jack. "You said you'd let us go on the tractors if we came to see you!"

"So, how's it going?" asked Aunt Thea while Jack and Lewis fidgeted behind her, longing to run off towards the rides and waiting to ask if they could.

"Well, you know," sighed Carol, stacking some more loaves on her table. "Not great. I don't think we'll last much longer. With all the flooding for the third year running, we just can't bring a decent crop in. I can't see how we can go on."

Aunt Thea used her kindest voice. "You never know, this last bit of summer sun might keep going. You might get a decent crop yet!"

"No, I really think we will have to sell the farm and give it all up," sighed Carol. "The bank wants us to pay them back the loan from last year – and we just haven't got the money. They've given us another six weeks to find it – but we haven't got anything. And I love that farm! My family's been there for centuries. . ." Her voice broke a little and Jack and Lewis

looked at each other, feeling bad for her.

"How about opening up to schools – becoming a visitor's farm?" suggested Aunt Thea.

"It's a nice idea," sniffed Carol. "But why would they come? What's special about a few fields and barns and livestock? We're just an ordinary working farm – not an exciting attraction, like kids want these days. No . . . I think it's all over."

"Go on, you two," said Aunt Thea, glancing at Jack and Lewis. "Go off to the rides. I'll find you in a while."

They sped off, relieved. "That's a bit sad for her, isn't it?" murmured Jack. "I'd love to have a farm. And I'd hate it if I had to lose it."

"Yeah," agreed Lewis. "Look! A big wheel!" He darted off to the little fairground and Jack ran after him.

The big wheel wasn't actually *that* big. It was a small, travelling fair, so it couldn't be huge. It was still as high as a house, though, and made Jack's heart race when he got into one of the little swinging pods and sat down next to Lewis. He wasn't a big fan of scary, fast rides. "Oh

 51

come *on*!" grinned Lewis when he noticed how tightly his big brother was holding the safety bar. "You were flying on a dragon last night!"

"Yes. And I fell off!" pointed out Jack. The ride lurched and stopped again to let a fair-haired girl on to the pod just below them. There were eight pods which could each seat two or three people. The girl glanced up and then waved at them.

"Look! It's Sarah Adams, from school!" said Lewis. They waved back.

"How you doing?" called up Sarah.

"Great!" called back Lewis, leaning over the edge of their pod and making it swing, so Jack grabbed even tighter on to the bar. "Jack fell off a dragon last night, though, into a garden full of monsters!"

Sarah laughed. "You and your monster games!" she said, shaking her head. "Sometimes I think you really believe they're real."

Jack and Lewis looked at each other with a guilty grin. It was particularly funny hearing Sarah say this, because she had *met* Electrotaur and Slashermite. And a host of other Taurs and

Mites. In fact, only weeks ago she had helped them fight the Finger-Knitting War which had almost wrecked their school.

She'd been told all about Merrion's Mead and how it came into Jack and Lewis's lives.

But she didn't remember a thing.

After all she'd done to help them, they still couldn't let her go around knowing the secrets of Tauronia – it was just too dangerous. So Slashermite had hypnotized her, and now, if she remembered anything at all, she thought it was all just a game Jack and Lewis made up. The boys, and Aunt Thea, still felt rather bad about this, but it was for the best.

The big wheel gave another lurch and Sarah squeaked and sat back in her seat. Suddenly the pod above Jack and Lewis swung violently back and forth and jeering "girly" shrieks came from it. Sarah looked up and narrowed her eyes at whoever was in it. The pod swung harder and a fit of belching could be heard. Then the sound of someone robustly breaking wind, followed by more mocking girly shrieks.

"Oh no," groaned Jack. "I don't believe it."

 53

"What? Who is it?" Lewis turned around to see, but couldn't.

"That belching – it's got to be Baz. . ." winced Jack. "And . . . if I'm not mistaken. . ." A spit missile suddenly shot down past them towards Sarah. ". . .yep! Mick the Spit."

"Stop it, you apes!" they heard Sarah shout. Now the ride was going. The pod above them continued to lurch and swing madly as Baz,

the school bully, and his dribblesome sidekick, Mick the Spit, messed about. Spit rained down on the other pods and hit Lewis's hand twice. He squawked with disgust. After half a turn the ride was stopped and the pair were kicked off by the operator. They ran off, making rude signs at him and everyone else on the ride, before tripping up a skinny kid who wandered haplessly into their path, eating a candyfloss.

The ride edged along and then stopped again, because Sarah had got out and asked to change pods. She climbed in with Jack and Lewis and then the ride got started again.

"Brilliant!" Jack said to her, as they glided up to the highest curve of the wheel, watching Baz and Mick chase the skinny kid into the prize-winning sausages tent. "You come out for a day to get away from stupid people like Baz and Mick – and they show up!"

Sarah nodded grimly, with a flick of her blonde ponytail. "They shouldn't be allowed out."

"Um," said Lewis. His eyes looked a little glassy.

"Now we'll have to spend our time watching

 55

out for them," grumbled Jack. "What's up, Lew? You getting motion sick? I thought that was *my* job!"

"Um," said Lewis, again. "I think there's someone else we might have to watch out for." He pointed a shaky finger as their pod began to descend again. Jack followed its direction to an area of grass just behind the hotdog stand by the trees where a small, gangly person moved in a strange wiggly, sprawly fashion.

"Oh. Looks like there's some kind of fancy dress thing going on somewhere," Sarah was saying. "Some kid's all dressed up like a sunflower!"

Jack and Lewis didn't reply. They were staring down, their faces struck by the Brick of Horror.

Trundling along at the edge of the fair, in broad daylight, without a care in the Overworld, was Flowertaur.

Chapter Eight

Horror in the House

"Stop! Stop! We have to get off!" bawled Jack as their pod neared the ground.

"Look, this isn't a bloomin' bus!" scowled the operator.

"My brother's going to be sick!" shouted Jack and Lewis made retching noises. The operator grumbled loudly but stopped the ride again. They all jumped off and ran towards the hotdog stand.

"What's going on?" puffed Sarah. "Why are we running?"

"We've seen someone we know," panted Jack, desperately searching for another glimpse of Flowertaur between the tents and rides. He couldn't see him behind the hotdog stand as they arrived there.

"You don't need to come with us," said Lewis, also looking anxiously back and forth. Where *was* his Taur?

"Well, I'm not going off on my own to bump into Baz and Mick," she said. "I'll hang out with you a bit longer."

"Whoa! No! Oh no!" yelled Jack, clapping his hands to his temples. He had just seen the back of Flowertaur's head, ducking down into the exit door of the Haunted House. This end of the little fair was pretty quiet – which was probably why the screaming and running hadn't started yet. That could change at any second. He grabbed Lew's arm and began to run. As they reached the Ghost Train, the man taking the money woke up with a start.

"Two please!" gasped Jack, shoving some coins at him.

"Three!" added Sarah, shoving more coins at him.

They clattered into the Haunted House at high speed and Jack felt absolutely terrified.

58

Not of the wet sponge on a stick which flipped down limply into his face, or the glowing skeleton which moved jerkily across the darkened room on a bit of clothes line. He was terrified of what would happen if Flowertaur got away from them, here, in a busy fair and market. There would be panic! And maybe – if Flowertaur was in the mood – carnage.

Lewis had drawn Flowertaur with the power to shoot deadly poison-tipped thorns. Luckily, Flowertaur was mostly quite cheerful and wouldn't *want* to kill anyone unless they annoyed him or unless Lewis, his creator, told him to. As long as he was happy and relaxed, everything might still be OK, Jack told himself.

"Who are we looking for?" whispered Sarah, with a giggle, just behind them. She clearly thought this was just a game and had no idea that they were stalking a deadly assassin.

"Him!" said Lewis, pulling aside the curtain into the next room – a badly painted torture chamber with a model executioner made from a shop dummy, whose axe went up and down

59

with a creak and a whine. Sitting next to it in a rocking chair was Flowertaur.

"Who – what – *is* that thing?" whispered Sarah, pushing through some rather irritating fake cobwebs.

"Flowertaur!" said Lewis. "What are you doing outside Tauronia?"

Flowertaur smiled up from his armchair and gave them all a leafy wave. They saw 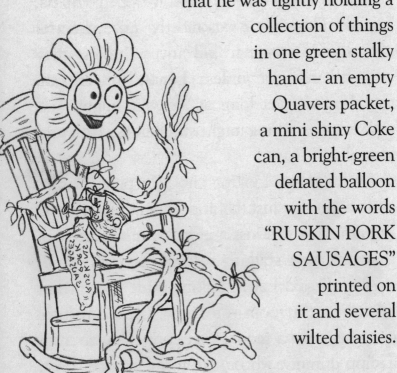 that he was tightly holding a collection of things in one green stalky hand – an empty Quavers packet, a mini shiny Coke can, a bright-green deflated balloon with the words "RUSKIN PORK SAUSAGES" printed on it and several wilted daisies.

"Flowertaur!" Lewis stood with his arms folded. "I said, what are you doing out here? You should be in Tauronia!"

Flowertaur stood up with a quiver of leaves. "Ma-aathh*ter*?" he lisped. Lewis blinked. He didn't remember giving his Taur such a strange and lispy voice, but he guessed he must have been thinking of it when he had drawn and meaded him.

"Well?" demanded Lewis. "What's going on? You should have gone back to Tauronia with the others last night."

"Otherth have gone baa-aack?" queried the floral being. "But what of our great quetht?"

"There is no quest," said Lewis. "It was a mistake. But even so, you should have waited in Aunt Thea's garden – not just gone off on a tour of the Overworld. It's very naughty! Don't you know how dangerous it is up here?"

Flowertaur gave them all a charming smile and fluttered his googly round eyes. "But Flowertaur jutht wanted to theee... Jutht wanted to ekthplore ... find pretty thingth..." He waved his odd collection of treasures.

"Has anyone seen you?" asked Jack. "Has there been any . . . screaming or running away or anything?" Flowertaur just smiled at him and slowly shook his head, the yellow petals around it waving gently. "And you haven't . . . you know . . . assassinated anyone?"

"I can't see any thorns missing," said Lewis. "I think we may just have got away with it."

"What *is* that?" asked Sarah.

"It's OK, he's a friend of ours," said Lewis. "I know he looks really weird, but he's all right."

"Where did he come from?"

"We'll explain it all to you later, if you promise to keep it secret," said Lewis.

Sarah nodded, her eyes still fixed on Flowertaur in amazement. "I feel like I've met him before," she murmured. She had.

"How will we get him back without being seen?" fretted Jack. "This is terrible! We haven't got any mead – we can't magic up an extra doorway to Tauronia. We can't get help from Electrotaur and Slashermite!"

"Slashermite?" muttered Sarah, nodding her head. "I know that name. Why do I know

62

that name?"

Jack was thinking hard, trying to work out a route back to Aunt Thea's car. He couldn't do it. "Lew!" he said. "We need your mapping brain! Quick! Think of the best way back to Aunt Thea's car – we can get him in the boot or something."

Lewis had the kind of brain which mapped things out very well. He always knew where he was going even if he'd been to a place only once before. He went to the window and yanked at the thick black sacking that was nailed across it. A bit of it came away and a shaft of light flooded through. Lewis pulled harder and the whole curtain ripped up the middle. He stuck his head out of the window and peered about. "OK," he said, pulling his head back in. "We've got to get him out of here and over to the trees. Then follow the trees back round to where the cars are parked. There's a kind of ditch, I think, that runs round. We should be able to go along that and keep down low."

"OK, that'll do for now," said Jack. "We've got to—"

There was a sudden crash against the wooden wall, just below the window.

Jack looked out and saw – oh no! – Baz and Mick the Spit, gurning up at him from below. They must have got bored with the candyfloss kid. Mick was chewing on an empty, pink-splodged stick.

"Oy! You! Come down 'ere!" shouted Baz.

"Push off," shouted back Jack. He hopped away from the window. "We've got trouble." He shook his head. "Big trouble."

Lewis bit his lip. He had recognized Baz's voice. "How are we going to get Flowertaur away now? He's going to get seen!"

"Don't worry. I'll distract them."

They looked around in surprise. Sarah was already turning to go.

"Wait!" hissed Jack. "We can't let you do that! They'll marmalize you!"

She grinned back at them over her shoulder. "No they won't," she said. "I can handle Baz and Mick . . . and I can run really fast too. You can't let them meet Flowertaur – they'll go nuts! I'll go and then you take him and run!"

She dashed over to the window. Baz and Mick were yelling cheery threats up at it and getting ready for a head-mashing session. Wet plops on the wood outside suggested that Mick was also doing some high velocity gobbing.

"Oy! Mick!" she yelled down to them. "Did you know that every time you spit, you lose five million brain cells? It explains a lot, doesn't it?"

Then she ducked back in and hared across to the stairs and down to the ground floor of the Haunted House, ignoring several fake spiders dangling on black wool and a flapping sheet which was meant to be a ghost. Seconds later, as Jack and Lewis poked their heads back through the ripped curtain, they saw her tearing across the grass, out in front where Baz and Mick could see her, waving and whooping at them. The boys immediately gave chase.

"Come on! We've got to go!" Lewis grabbed hold of Flowertaur's nearest tendril and yanked him out of the little room and over to the stairs.

But Jack was staring out of the window, aghast. "We can't leave her! We can't let her get caught by Baz and Mick!"

"She's fine!" yelled Lewis. "We've got to GO!"

He was right. Glancing out once more, Jack saw that Sarah was making a good getaway, sprinting back towards the Farmer's Market tents, Baz and Mick trailing behind. She turned to make a rude gesture at them, just to keep them coming.

"Come *on*!" Lewis called. "NOW! We have to run for it NOW!"

Chapter Nine

Ditchy and Scratchy

Lewis dragged Flowertaur across the patch of grass behind the Haunted House at top speed. Although he had a weird, flolloping, trundly way of moving, the Taur was quite fast. As they reached the cover of the trees Lewis yanked his leafy creation across a patch of weeds and brambles and then shoved him into the ditch, jumping down behind him and crouching low.

Jack arrived seconds later.

"Did anyone see us?" gasped Lewis, his heart racing, still holding firmly on to Flowertaur to stop him from bobbing his big flowery head up above the brambles.

Jack shook his head. "No, I don't think so.

There were some more kids going into the Haunted House, so the funfair bloke wasn't watching. Eeeuw." He looked down to see a muddy rivulet of water seeping into his trainers.

"OK, now we just have to go along here, round in a big curve, and climb up out of the ditch again when we're by the car park," said Lewis. "This way." He led Flowertaur along, keeping his knees bent and his head down. Jack followed, doing the same. Flowertaur also kept his head down, seeming to understand that they must keep hidden.

The ditch was filled with rubbish and weeds and after a while it sank lower into the earth until its sides were about as tall as Jack. Sometimes brambles grew right across it over their heads and caught in their hair or scratched their foreheads. Their feet squelched as they picked their way along.

"Oh *great*," muttered Lewis. Up ahead the ditch went into a short concrete pipe where a gravel track went across above it.

When they got to it he could see that kids had tried to make a den here. There were some

cardboard boxes and some mould-covered cushions off a sofa. Empty drinks cans lay in the water in the bottom curve of the pipe. There was a rusty bike chain and an old upturned buggy near the other end. The buggy was actually in quite good condition, Lewis noted, as they passed it. All four wheels were still on it.

"Uugh!" coughed Jack, as something scuttled between his feet. "A rat!"

"Cool!" said Lewis, his voice odd and echoey. He liked rats.

"Come on, let's get out of here. It's creepy!" Jack gave Flowertaur a nudge from behind, careful to avoid a thorny bit of him. The Taur's body was exactly like a very thick stem of rose bush. He turned his weird smiley face back at Jack and gave him a rather scary grin before trundling on after Lewis.

"Nearly there," Lewis said, reaching the other end of the pipe. "The ditch isn't that deep now, so we'll have to keep low. Better wait here with Flowertaur and let me check there's nobody about." He let go of Flowertaur and

 69

ran the last few metres. He popped his head out of the pipe and glanced left and right. Nobody. Phew! They still had a bit further to go along the ditch, before they reached the car park.

He turned back to call the others out but just as he opened his mouth there was a wet plop on top of his head. "Wha—?" he gasped and stared up. Leaning over the ledge above the pipe outlet were Baz and Mick the Spit. Mick was working his mouth left and right, building up another saliva missile. Baz was grinning and holding a muddy old boot.

"Oy!" he shouted, before hurling the boot hard at Lewis's head. "Present for you!"

The boot struck Lewis hard on the head, making him stagger and fall back into the ditch. Jack suddenly shot out of the pipe, spinning round to see his brother's attackers. He had a chunk of rotten wood in his hand and he threw it up at Mick with all his might. The edge of it thunked into Mick's ribs, but didn't seem to bother the boy, who just spat down a big foamy lump which hit Jack's arm.

Then the stones came. The pair had a little pile of them on the ledge they were perched on and with whoops of glee they began to pelt them down at Jack and Lewis. Jack was filled with fury. He tried to stand in front of his brother. *Crack!* A stone hit his pocket. His glasses were inside it. It sounded like a lens had broken.

"Knock it OFF!" he yelled out.

Another chunk of stone hit Lewis hard on the shin. Jack ran towards the ledge and tried to leap up and catch Baz's foot – to unbalance him and get him to fall off. But Baz saw it coming and kicked his foot hard down on to Jack's head. Jack fell back,

dazed, with a whump, on to the concrete. Now Lewis was on his feet again, trying to throw the fallen stones back up at Baz and Mick.

Then there was a pause in the noise. Jack, still on his back, his vision cloudy, felt his skin prickle with horror. Something green and leafy had just swept over his shoulder. Flowertaur had trundled out of the pipe and turned to face the enemy above them.

"What is THAT?" gasped Baz, his hand, clutching a stone, paused in the air as he took in the full floral weirdness of the Taur.

"I – I – I dunno. . ." whined Mick.

Jack was suddenly struck with a terrible thought. "Don't *move!*" he called out. "Whatever you do – DON'T MOVE!"

For a few seconds, as Flowertaur stared up at them, his long tendrils quivering with tense fury, it seemed as if Mick and Baz were doing as Jack had told them. They were frozen with shock. But then it went wrong. Very wrong.

72

"Gob on *this*!" squawked Mick. "Let's geddit!" And he threw a large rock at Flowertaur.

Flowertaur's nearest leafy limb shot up and deflected the rock, but then the next one went wide and hit Lewis. Instantly, Flowertaur shot out a wiry green creeper at incredible speed, which wrapped itself around Mick's waist and then flicked him down on to the floor in front of them with a crack. Then the green creeper thumped him up and down two or three times. Mick squealed, his head flipping about and his eyes bulging so wide they looked like ping-pong balls. Above him, Baz was grunting, "WOT? WOT? WOT? WOT?" his face scarlet with fear. Then he raised a very large lump of concrete in both hands and ran along to the far edge of the ledge, the better to chuck it down on Lewis.

And this was his mistake. Aiming for Lewis was a very bad idea.

Very.

Flowertaur whipped around to face the

 73

concrete-wielding thug and then, just as Lewis screamed "FLOWERTAUR – NOOOOO!" there were several "thwip" noises. Poison-tipped thorns shot through the air like bullets.

A second later, Baz hit the ground like a wet sack of cement.

Chapter Ten

Buggy with a Baz on Top

Jack could not believe how awful this day was turning out to be. An escaped Taur in the Overworld was dreadful. And now Baz lay at his feet, distinctly dead. Which was just beyond words.

There was a squeak above him and he looked up to see Mick running away at top speed, gibbering.

"What are we going to do?" he breathed, as they stared back at Baz, lying still on the floor. Lewis gulped and then stepped across to prod the back of Baz's head. Jack closed his eyes in horror. "Is he . . . dead?"

Lewis gulped. "Those thorns are tipped with deadly poison and he got a load of them."

Jack found his feet and sprang across to Baz. He rolled the boy over. Baz's eyes were fixed open and he was dribbling. "He's not dead!" Jack let out a huge sigh of relief.

"But he *will* be," said Lewis, again. He looked white and scared. "Soon. I know that poison. I thought it up. It's the making things dead kind."

"We've got to get him to Aunt Thea! Now!" said Jack.

Lewis looked around and saw Flowertaur was leaning against the edge of the concrete pipe, polishing the thorns on his fingertips. "You!" he said. "Do exactly what I say, or I'll rub you out next time I get to my drawings!"

"Of courshe, mashter," simpered Flowertaur

with a sickly smile.

"Go and get the buggy!" ordered Lewis and Flowertaur did so, returning a few seconds later and plonking it down next to Baz's feet.

Lewis had carefully collected all the deadly thorns off Baz, and was poking them deep into the mud, out of harm's way. "Only two got through to his skin, I think," he said. "The one on his neck went the deepest. And one was in his ear. The others just got stuck in his clothes."

He and Jack struggled to get the well-built Baz off the floor, but eventually, with much straining and grunting, they managed to get him into the buggy. His chunky bottom only just squeezed into the seat, but at least the tight fit meant he'd be less likely to tumble out. Jack picked up the boy's feet and jammed them back on to the rusty little footrest, and his knees went up almost as high as his ears. Through all of this, Baz only dribbled and stared. He made no noise at all, and he was turning yellow.

"Is he still alive?" gulped Jack, surveying their passenger.

"Yes," said Lewis. "He's only yellow. When he goes orange . . . well . . . come on! We have to go!" He turned to Flowertaur. "You will stay in the pipe until we come for you," he said, in as masterly a voice as he could manage. "Do you understand me?"

"Yeshth, masther," said Flowertaur and backed into the pipe until he was out of sight.

Somehow, Jack and Lewis managed to drag the half-dead bully in the buggy up out of the ditch and on to the small gravel track above, which led through the trees in one direction, and across the bottom end of the recreation park towards some changing rooms and, finally, the car park, in the other direction. They began to run towards the changing rooms, pushing the buggy with all their strength, at top speed, and praying that the wheels wouldn't fall off. It was a bit wonky, but seemed to be fairly robust.

Lewis kept looking around for Mick, but there was no sign of the boy at all. He hoped he wouldn't suddenly show up with some grown-ups, demanding to know who'd tried to kill Baz. Worse still, if anyone went back to the ditch and looked in the pipe. . .

"Oh, why did you have to make him an assassin?" wailed Jack as they ran.

"Well I didn't know he was going to start roaming the Overworld and bumping off our enemies, did I?" retorted Lewis. "And *I* didn't let him out of Tauronia! And why didn't Sortitoutataur get him back home, eh? *You* drew Sortitoutataur, didn't you?! So it was *your* Taur who messed up on that!"

Jack frowned. He remembered telling Sortitoutataur to get all the Taurs and Mites out of Aunt Thea's garden and back down to Tauronia – which his creation had done. Flowertaur must have already escaped the garden, and so he was not included in the instruction. Sortitoutataur had done exactly what he was told to. He wasn't asked to get every Taur that had *escaped* back home – only those in Aunt Thea's garden. That's why Stinkermite, Electrotaur and Slashermite, all sitting in the house, hadn't returned. With a chill, Jack wondered if any *other* Taurs or Mites had escaped the clear-up.

 79

They ran on, with Baz's knees thunking left and right and his yellow head lolling sideways. As they tore around the bend in the path past the changing rooms, a lady and her dog were coming in the other direction. They nearly collided with her. "Sorry!" cried Lewis.

"My goodness! Is that boy all right?" gasped the woman, as she reined in her terrier on its lead. "He's awfully yellow."

"He's not a boy!" spluttered Jack, trying to get the buggy moving again, while Baz's head started to tip over and his yellow tongue lolled out of his mouth. "He's . . . he's a. . ."

"GUY!" shouted Lewis. "He's our Guy Fawkes!"

The woman looked uncertain as they ran on past her. But she blinked and patted her coat pocket. "Oh," she laughed. "I haven't got my glasses on again! Gosh! He really does look like a boy, you know! A rather yellow one. . ."

"Yeah, well . . . we made his head out of a melon," hazarded Jack, over his shoulder, as they steered the buggy on.

"Oh well, I hope you get plenty of pennies,"

called the woman and went on her way.

A few seconds later Jack commented, "A good job she didn't remember that November the fifth is still weeks away."

They reached the car park and came to a halt by Aunt Thea's black VW Beetle. "One of us is going to have to run and find Aunt Thea," Jack said.

Lewis stared anxiously at Baz's face. It wasn't orange yet – but the yellow was much more yellowy. Baz's head, with its close cropped mousy hair, was beginning to look like a large round cheese. His little brown eyes stared out of it, dazed and dull. Lewis tried to poke his tongue back in, as flies kept settling on it.

"He looks done for," he said. "If I can just get to the magic mead in time I can make an antidote. But I reckon he's only got a few minutes. Look. His ears are going orange."

Jack shook his head in dismay. Baz was doomed. How were they ever going to explain this? Of all the calamities that Merrion's Mead had brought about, this was the worst!

Then there was a shout and two figures were

racing across the car park towards them – Sarah and Aunt Thea.

"Are you both all right?!" yelled Aunt Thea, skidding to a halt as Jack ran to meet her. "Sarah said Flowertaur was loose in the Overworld – and you were being chased by bullies – is this true? Don't tell me they saw Flowertaur!"

"Erm – well," said Jack, leading them back towards the buggy. "Flowertaur made a bit of an impression on Baz."

Aunt Thea took a look at Baz in his buggy and groaned with horror.

"He and Mick the Spit were chucking stones at Lewis and Flowertaur got angry. . ." explained Jack.

"Come on!" said Aunt Thea, unlocking the Beetle door. "I've got emergency mead in the car. Oh my word, I hope we're not too late."

Jack and Lewis ran the buggy around to the side of the Beetle. Thankfully it was parked in a remote corner of the car park. Aunt Thea got the passenger door open and they tipped the buggy up. Baz thudded face first on to the passenger seat.

"The mead! The mead!" yelled Jack. "Quick!"

Aunt Thea dug inside her glove compartment and thrust a woody bottle at Jack, and a notepad and pencil at Lewis, who leaned on the bonnet of the Beetle and scribbled something very, very fast. Then Jack sploshed some mead on to Lewis's scribbling. Then Lewis grabbed the bottle from him and sploshed more mead on to Baz's head.

Then they waited, breathless with fear. Baz's whole face was orange beneath the drops of mead. There was no getting away from it.

"I think we're too late," murmured Jack, running his hands through his hair.

"No! We can't be!" Lewis gave Baz's shoulder

 83

a shake. "I made it so that Merrion's Mead itself is an antidote. It was the quickest thing I could think of. It's magic. It's *got* to save him."

Sarah leaned into the car behind Jack. "So Baz and Mick came back for you! I thought they might when they gave up chasing me. I saw your aunt, so I told her everything and we came running back to the car to get the mead so you could make Flowertaur go home."

"How did you know Aunt Thea?" wondered Jack. He and Aunt Thea exchanged glances.

"The hypnotism obviously wasn't strong enough," said Aunt Thea. "After seeing Flowertaur, Sarah's memory has started to come back."

"Ah," said Jack.

"*What* hypnotism?" asked Sarah, looking confused.

"YES!" Lewis patted Baz's cheeks, which had now gone back to yellow. As they watched they could see the yellow fading and Baz's more normal skin colour returning.

"Right!" said Aunt Thea. "Now we have to deposit this boy somewhere safe before he properly wakes up."

"Shouldn't we get him back to Slashermite for hypnotism?" asked Jack .

"Wait," said Lewis. He scribbled something else through the damp mead on the notebook. "I've made it so the antidote makes people relax and forget about Flowertaur too."

"Right, good thinking!" said Aunt Thea. "Now, let's dump him over on one of the benches by the changing rooms. He can sleep it off."

Keeping an eye out for passers-by, they trundled Baz back along the path. And just as they turned the corner by the changing rooms block, Mick suddenly ran right into them. He squawked with shock and fear when he saw Baz, but as soon as he opened his mouth to shout, Jack, still clutching the little wooden bottle, uncorked it and shook some Merrion's Mead into his face. Mick immediately went quiet and dreamy and sat down. They propped the pair of them together on the bench.

Baz cuddled up to dopey Mick, dribbling. He seemed to be having quite a nice dream. "Jam please, Mum," he said, sweetly, as everyone tiptoed away.

 85

Flowertaur was still in the pipe as promised when they got back. Lewis didn't say anything else to him. He just drew Flowertaur in his pad, wrote "Returns home to Tauronia imeedietly" next to it, then dropped some more mead on to it. Flowertaur vanished with a *pop* and they all breathed a sigh of relief.

"Sarah, would you like to come to my cottage for tea, today?" said Aunt Thea, briskly, as they walked back to the fair and the Farmer's Market stalls.

"I'll ask Mum, she's in the cheese tent," said Sarah. "Why? Are you going to tell me more secrets about Tauronia?"

"Yes," said Aunt Thea, with a warm smile. "We'll fill your head with the whole amazing story."

She didn't add "Then we'll empty it all out again." But the guilty look she shot Jack and Lewis said it loud and clear.

Chapter Eleven

A Bit Pressed

"What a day!" said Aunt Thea as she set a plate of cupcakes down on the table and went to put the kettle on. "Thank goodness it's all over!" She had just got off the phone to Carol, who had not managed to sell very much at the Farmer's Market that morning.

"Poor Carol. She's having such a bad time," she told her nephews as Lewis struggled not to grab a cupcake. "She's already asked an estate agent up to value the farm. I think it will break her heart to sell it. I wish there was something I could do to help."

"We could try drawing some money and meading it to life!" offered Lewis, but Aunt Thea smiled and patted his head. "I don't think you really could, Lewis. It probably wouldn't quite pass for *real* money. You're a very clever boy, but not an expert in banknote forgery."

The doorbell chimed. "Ah, that'll be Sarah," said Aunt Thea. "Now, boys, don't be soft. You know what we have to do after tea." Sarah's mum had said yes to the visit. She knew Jack and Lewis's mum quite well, so was happy for Sarah to visit her school friends and their aunt.

The day had grown dark and cloudy although it was only half past four. When she opened her door, Aunt Thea was surprised to see that one of her neighbours stood on her front step, rather than Sarah.

"Oh, hello, Mrs Peebles," said Aunt Thea. "What can I do for you?"

The old lady pulled her beige cardigan tightly round her chest and nodded upwards, her eyes sliding skywards. "I was just wondering, dear," she said, "what *that* is."

Aunt Thea blinked with surprise and then stepped out of the door, turned around and looked up, following Mrs Peebles' line of sight.

88

Then she gulped. High above her roof, a clear beam of blue light was dissecting the low grey cloud.

"Is it a laser show?" asked Mrs Peebles. "I've seen these laser show things on the telly. It's a bit of a dull one, if it is. Just shines up, straight as a ruler. Nothing much else doing. But it *is* coming from your garden, isn't it?"

"Well, er. . ." Aunt Thea squirmed, wondering what to say. She was aghast. The standing stone was still shining its light up into space. It *had* faded with the dawn, but now she realized it had probably been going all day but wasn't visible in daylight. Now, as the dark clouds rolled in, it was *very* visible. "It's – er – it's—"

"My experiment!" chimed in a cheery young voice. Aunt Thea took a deep breath and gave silent thanks. Jack came out of the front door and smiled at Mrs Peebles. And now Sarah was coming up the path, waving goodbye as her mother's car pulled away.

"What do you think?" said Jack to Mrs Peebles. "It's a really strong torch and I've put loads of batteries in it and I have to time how long they

 89

last. And then I try cheaper batteries and see how long *they* last and so on. Then I calculate the difference in price and work out the value of the power units in the batteries and—"

"All right, all right, young man! I get the drift," said Mrs Peebles. "Mighty powerful torch, though, I must say."

"Yes it is," said Jack, flicking a glance at Aunt Thea who was shrugging and pulling faces at him over Mrs Peebles' shoulder.

"Well, I hope you don't intend to do your experiment all week long, young man," went on Mrs Peebles. "That's light pollution, that is! Might confuse pilots in aeroplanes!"

"Oh, I'm sure the batteries won't last much longer, Mrs Peebles," said Aunt Thea. "Now, come along in, you two. Tea is ready." Jack beckoned Sarah inside but Mrs Peebles wasn't in any hurry to depart. She loitered on the front path, still staring up, and then dropped her gaze to peer hard at her neighbour.

"Um. . . Was there anything else?" asked Aunt Thea.

Mrs Peebles sniffed. She dug a crumpled grey

hanky out of her cardigan sleeve and mopped at her nose before replying. "Some say," she said, "*that the truth is out there!*"

"I'm sorry?" Aunt Thea tilted her head and peered back at Mrs Peebles. "What truth? Out where?"

"Aliens," answered Mrs Peebles. "Up there in the sky. Or maybe. . ." she looked darkly across her hanky, ". . .down here!"

"What *do* you mean?" queried Aunt Thea.

"Well, there was that dragon sighting last night, for one thing! And then the little green man. . ."

"Dragon? Little green *man*? Really, Mrs Peebles."

"No, it's true! Gracie Lewis saw it by her pond! A skinny green man with a big head. And a little blue creature, leaping over the Joneses' chimney stack. A little blue alien from Mercury and a little green alien from Mars."

"Are you sure Gracie Lewis wasn't having a little joke?" asked Aunt Thea, feeling distinctly nervous.

"She crossed her heart!" said Mrs Peebles

with a grave nod. "Aliens, I tell you! Checking us out. And if you start shining lights up in the sky, who's to say they won't think it's a sign? A beacon! Just you think on that!"

"Well," Aunt Thea began to close her door. "Thanks for the advice. I will certainly bear it in mind."

Mrs Peebles at last turned away. "I know all about it. I've seen it on the telly," she said, as she wandered slowly down the path. "It's all a big cover-up. Someone should call someone. . . There's alien hunters up the road at Stonehenge this *week*, you know. They're always looking out for flying saucers – they think Stonehenge is one great big welcome mat for Martians, that's what they think."

Aunt Thea closed the door and walked swiftly into the kitchen where Jack and Lewis and Sarah were opening the back door and heading out into the garden. "The blue beam is still here!" Lewis was marvelling.

"Well done for thinking up that cover story so fast, Jack." Aunt Thea patted her nephew on the shoulder as they all hurried up the garden.

"I was clean out of ideas! That's all we need – Mrs Peebles! That woman could win Olympic gold for gossip. She says one of our neighbours 'saw aliens' in her garden – a green one with a big head and a blue one."

As they reached the standing stone, she fixed Lewis and Jack with a hard stare. "We know who the green one with the big head was – Flowertaur. And he's dealt with. But what about the blue one?"

Jack and Lewis looked at each other and then back at Aunt Thea and shrugged. "Can't think of a blue one," said Jack. "She might just have seen Flowertaur again in the moonlight. I'm sure all the others went home."

Aunt Thea shook her head. "Well, I hope you're right. Maybe we should ask Slashermite to check that everyone's arrived back, though, to be sure. It's really so worrying – but for now, we have a more urgent problem. We've got to stop that light." She had picked up some thick navy cushions from the garden swing as they passed, and now reached up and put them on top of the stone, over the source of the light.

93

For a few seconds it looked as if this had cut off the blue glow – but then the light began to push its way through the cushions, no matter how thick and dark they were.

"Well, it's magic light, all right," sighed Aunt Thea. "A normal light couldn't do that! It must be connected to the lightning strike which opened it up last night . . . but why is it still shining after we've sent all the Taurs and Mites back to Tauronia? Surely any Tauronian energy should have gone back with them after Sortitoutataur did his thing?"

"Let's get Slashermite up to ask if he knows anything about it," said Lewis.

"Ah, yes," said Aunt Thea, eyeing Sarah. "We need to get Slashermite up for a couple of things."

"*Now* I remember!" Sarah was saying, as she stared at the standing stone. She traced its speckly red and black surface with her fingertips. "This is the Gateway to Tauronia! It *is* real! It *is*! How could I forget?"

"Well, erm," said Jack, looking rather flushed. "You've only seen it once, after . . . er . . . all that business in the playground with. . ."

94

"The attack of the finger-knitting!" squeaked Sarah. "Everyone got smothered in big woolly creepers of finger-knitting! And then Floatingfrostataur froze everyone! And then Sortitoutataur sorted everything out and. . ." She wrinkled up her brow. "That's all I can remember. . ."

"Well, no need to worry your head about that now," said Aunt Thea, briskly. "Lewis, can you nip back inside and mead up Slashermite?"

Five minutes later, a doorway appeared at the back of the standing stone and Slashermite scampered out of it, his finger-blades wiggling with excitement. He loved coming up to the garden to play. Normally they would have called up Electrotaur too, as he was Slashermite's best friend and Jack's most important Taur. As both monsters were the first ever to come to life, they knew Jack, Lewis and Aunt Thea very well. They were reliable and brave, even if Electrotaur was somewhat unfriendly.

But although Slashermite was delighted to be up in the Overworld again, he could not come up with any ideas about why the

95

light was still beaming up out of the standing stone.

"It is a mystery!" he marvelled, gazing up at it and carefully scratching his purple ear in wonder. "I have asked many Taurs and Mites – but we know nothing of this."

"Are you sure?" asked Jack. "Did you ask Stinkermite and Lavataur and Dragotaur? Did any of them even know about the blue light?"

"I am sorry, but no, Master Jack. There has been much talk of The Great Quest That Never Was," he added, giving them all a rather reproving look, "and the excitement of the visit to the

Overworld – but nobody can explain the blue light."

They went back into the house to have scones, jam, cream and tea. And special porridge for Slashermite with chocolate sugar strands dropped into it to look like ants. Ant porridge was his favourite thing to eat. Lewis had made that up before he'd accidentally brought Slashermite to life. The first time Slashermite had eaten porridge it had indeed had real ants in it. Jack and Lewis felt guilty about that to this day. Happily Lewis's Mite seemed just as content with the vegetarian version.

"OK, let's be logical about this. Someone, somewhere, *has* to know what that light is all about," reasoned Aunt Thea, splodging a thick blob of clotted cream on top of the jam on her scone. "Slashermite, I am sorry to go on about this, but I must be sure. What about Tundrataur?" Slashermite shook his head, smiling apologetically around a mouth full of porridge. "Mechanitaur? The Jellymites? Ninjataur?"

"No, Lady Thea. Nobody I have asked knows anything of the blue light. But I haven't asked all of them yet. Flowertaur has only just come back – *bad Taur!*" Slashermite looked fiercely disapproving. "And Ninjataur I have not seen since last night. Although he is not easily seen at any time. He is a *Ninja*taur, after all. He sometimes climbs up my castle walls and I never know about it, until he appears next to me from nowhere. It is impolite."

Lewis grinned. He had drawn Ninjataur after watching a film about the legendary silent, deadly Japanese warriors. Ninjataur was dressed from head to foot in soft silk, the colour of the night sky, his face swathed in a bandage-like blue scarf with his glittery silver eyes peering through a gap, and his feet in soft navy blue boots. He kept a ninjato short sword at his waist for defence, but never needed it. He could move and jump and climb so stealthily and so fast, he was impossible to catch. He liked to tease the other Mites and Taurs – especially the big violent ones like Grippakillataur. Ninjataur was such a cool Taur, thought Lewis. A sudden uneasiness washed over him, making his grin fade. But no – he was sure Ninjataur would show up in Tauronia soon.

"Right, here's what we'd like you to do," Aunt Thea told Slashermite. "When you've finished your porridge, please pop back down to Tauronia and take a register. Get Electrotaur to help you. And make sure that everyone who should be there *is* there – and that you've definitely asked them all about the blue light. Can you do that?"

Slashermite nodded eagerly. "Yes! Every Taur or Mite created by the masters is listed on the plinth of the statue of the creators in Tauronia Town Square. Also the two made by you, Lady Thea. I engrave their names myself, as soon as a new creation arrives."

He flexed his finger-blades proudly. "I will call a meeting and we will take a register!"

"Yeah, well, don't worry if Invisitaur or the Hero don't turn up," muttered Aunt Thea. "You know my creations can't always manage their existence terribly well." Poor Aunt Thea had drawn and meaded a couple of creatures of her own some time back but they tended to flicker in and out of being. This was because Aunt Thea, being grown-up, just could not *totally* believe in them – no matter how hard she tried.

Slashermite finished up his porridge and went swiftly back to Tauronia to carry out his quest.

As they sat back, full of tea, Sarah said, "Look, can you just fill me in about Tauronia? I keep remembering things but forgetting why I forgot them in the first place."

"Don't worry," said Aunt Thea. "When Slashermite comes back we can explain it all to you and then . . . and then set your mind at rest."

Jack and Lewis looked at each other. They knew what that meant. Aunt Thea was determined to get Sarah hypnotized to forget again. She would insist that it was for the best. Knowing about Tauronia could be a very dangerous thing. Their cousin once very nearly got eaten because of it.

"Anyway," went on Aunt Thea, but then

her phone rang so she got up to answer it. "Hello? Who? Oh, really? Um . . . no. No, I wasn't aware of that. Look, can you hold on a minute?" She put her hand over the receiver and stared around at them all. "It's a reporter!" she hissed. "Someone called Chris Cooper, from *The Journal*! Asking about the blue light!"

Jack jumped up and pressed the loudspeaker button on Aunt Thea's phone. She went back to the reporter. "Sorry about that – what were you saying?"

"Well, Miss Casterbridge," said the reporter. His voice sounded tinny through the phone's small speaker. "I know it seems silly, but we've had a call from one of your neighbours, telling us there's a kind of laser light shining up out of your garden, from an ancient standing stone. Is that right?"

"Well, er, in a manner of speaking," said Aunt Thea. "But it's nothing sinister. Just my nephew's science experiment. Just a torch, you know."

"Well, yes, I thought that it was probably something like that," said the reporter. "Only . . .

101

it does seem like rather a powerful light for just a torch."

"It's a BIG torch," snapped Aunt Thea. "And anyway, how do you know how powerful it is?"

"Well, I'm in the car with a photographer, just outside," explained the reporter.

"Good lord, haven't you got anything better to do?" Aunt Thea spluttered. "Surely there's a murder trial or something for you to cover?"

The reporter chuckled. "I know it's all probably nothing but after the report of the dragon in last night's storm and then the alleged alien sightings, well . . . we've got to check these things out. Even if it's only a bit of fun. Can we come in? We'll be right across."

"What? No! No, you can't come in," shouted Aunt Thea, but the reporter had already ended the call. Seconds later there was a knock at the door. "Go away!" yelled Aunt Thea. "It's not convenient! I have guests."

"All we want is a photo," called the reporter through the letterbox. "Just a shot of your nephew's torch experiment . . . so we can run a funny on it! You know, how hilarious it was that all your neighbours were thinking of UFOs and all that! Once they see the torch, they'll know how silly they've been."

Aunt Thea ran into the front room. She peered carefully through the net curtains as Lewis, Jack and Sarah crowded behind her. A knot of six or seven neighbours was outside by the fence, eagerly watching the reporter and the photographer next to him, who was fitting a long lens on to his camera.

"Oh no," moaned Aunt Thea. "Now what do we do?"

Chapter Twelve

Extwob and The Beeb

"Go away! No comment!" bellowed Aunt Thea, for the fifteenth time. The reporter was nothing if not persistent. He had been on their doorstep for an hour now, pleading, persuading and cajoling through the letterbox. The photographer was no longer with him. He had gone next door and persuaded Aunt Thea's neighbour to let him lean precariously out of her bathroom window to take photos of the standing stone. Lewis found this out when he went outside to investigate the flashes.

"Oh, this is so not good," moaned Aunt Thea, slumped against the kitchen door. She had shut it tight against the continual pestering from the front step. "What are we going to *do*?"

"Can't we get help from the magic mead somehow?" asked Jack. "Get Sortitoutataur up or something?"

"Yes, of course," said Aunt Thea, getting to her feet. "We can just get him to stop the light! Then these people would all go away. Draw him right here in the kitchen again – we can't collect him from the gateway."

Jack already had the drawer open and was pulling out the folder with all their Taur and Mite pictures in it. He found the latest sketch of Sortitoutataur and hastily meaded it. With a click, the Taur arrived, looking weary.

"OK, *now* what?" he said.

"Please, Sortitoutataur, can you stop the blue light shining up out of the standing stone?" asked Jack. "And hurry!"

Sortitoutaur walked to the window, stared up the garden, and made a bit of a straining noise. "Well," he said, after a few seconds. "It's . . . gone." He didn't sound very sure. They all ran to the window and gazed up into the sky above the standing stone.

"Woo hoo! It's. . ." Jack tailed off. ". . .not

quite gone." Certainly the blue light was not so bright and at first glance it did look as if it had gone, but now it was beginning to shine brightly again.

"What's wrong?" asked Aunt Thea. "Why hasn't it gone, Sortitoutataur?"

"Well, I don't know. . ." shrugged the Taur. "I sorted it out – and then it just came back again. It's not *my* fault."

"Try again," said Jack.

Sortitoutataur sighed heavily and then made the straining noise again. For a second time the light vanished, but almost instantly it began to gently glow and build up again.

"I can't undo it," said Sortitoutataur. He pursed his pencil-thin lips. "It's been done with very strong magic. Only whoever made it happen will be able to make it un-happen."

"You really mean it?" asked Jack. "You can't sort it out?"

"I'm not a miracle worker, you know!" snapped Sortitoutataur.

"OK, well, thanks for trying. You can go home now," said Jack and his creation popped out of sight, leaving a burnt paper smell in the air. "Now what?" he said, while Aunt Thea and Lewis stared out through the kitchen window with renewed anxiety.

"Um – everyone. . ." Sarah called from the front room, where she was stationed by the window, peering between the drawn curtains. "More people!"

Aunt Thea, Jack and Lewis joined her and peered through the crack in the curtains. There were around twenty people milling around in the road outside, and the reporter was on the front step, talking into his mobile phone. As they stared out in appalled wonder, a large white van with a metal dish on its roof pulled up, scattering the crowd. It had BBC written on the side.

"I don't believe this!" murmured Aunt Thea. "The BBC? Whatever *next*?"

The phone went once again in the kitchen and once again they let the answering machine get it, although they all wandered back in to stare anxiously at it. The volume was left up so they could hear the messages. Chris Cooper from

The Journal had left about fifteen now. This time a new voice came through the speaker.

"Miss Casterbridge, I do apologize," came the well-spoken BBC voice of a young woman. "This must seem like an absolute circus out here, and the last thing I want to do is add to your troubles."

"Not *much*," muttered Aunt Thea.

"My name's Laura and I work for BBC TV. The regional news programme. We've heard about the light from the stone and we would be very happy to help you debunk this whole alien story and set the record straight. We're sure there is a perfectly normal explanation for the light – and the sightings."

"If that's so, why are you here, miss?" asked Aunt Thea.

"Laura! Laura who?" asked Sarah, running to stare at the machine as if its digital display could tell her.

"Please call me. I'm Laura Trant and you can reach me on—"

"That's my cousin!" squeaked Sarah. "Laura! She works on TV!"

"Jolly good for her," snapped Aunt Thea.

"She's really nice!"

"I'm sure she is."

"She might be able to help us," insisted Sarah.

"How, exactly? By broadcasting my back garden live to the south of England?"

"Well, maybe if I went out and spoke to her and said it was all a big mistake and just an experiment and all that, she might believe me and tell all the others and they'd all go away."

Aunt Thea sighed. "Sarah, she's a journalist! She won't just take anyone's word for it. She'll want to have a look. I know! I'm a journalist myself, of sorts. Although I do travel writing and don't need to go door-stepping defenceless strangers to earn my wage. But *I* would never take anybody's word for something when I could check it out myself."

"I know!" Jack suddenly leaped up from the sofa. "Let's set it up! Let's take some torches out there and put them up on the stone and make it *look* like it's just the torches! You've got some in the cellar, haven't you?"

109

"But Jack, the photographer's already got shots of it from next door's bathroom!" wailed Aunt Thea.

"But he can't be *that* close up, can he? You can't see all of it from there — there's bushes in the way. We can make out that we've sort of reflected it from lower down or something. I mean, all we have to do is convince Sarah's cousin and then she'll go and tell all the others and, well, she's from the BBC. They're bound to believe *her*!"

Aunt Thea considered this for a moment. "Well. . . It's worth a try. And I can't come up with a better idea. OK, go and get some torches and, yes, some blue paper. I have shiny blue wrapping paper that should do it. And some mirrors. We can make out it's being reflected. . . But how can we get up the garden and sort it out with that photographer watching?"

"Can't we just draw some torches and stuff and mead it?" asked Lewis.

"No," said Aunt Thea, firmly. "There's been far too much magic stuff going on in the real world as it is . . . and in any case, that standing stone isn't playing by the rules! I wouldn't bet on anything we put near it with magic mead coming out right just now. No, you and Jack will have to take real torches and stuff up there – and find a way not to get papped."

"Papped?" echoed Sarah.

"Photographed by paparazzi photographers! The *press*!"

"Aunty, you'll have to create a distraction!" said Lewis. "You'll have to go out and talk to them and make a big fuss, so the photographer will come out of the bathroom next door and get down in front of the house."

"Good thinking," said Aunt Thea. "Well. . ." she gulped, as Jack ran back in with the torches and a roll of blue wrapping paper. "If there's one thing I know how to do, it's create a distraction."

She took a deep breath and then strode to the front door.

Aunt Thea opened the door and a bright white

111

light shone in her eyes. She screwed up her face and put up her hands to shield herself. As she got used to the glare, she realized it was coming from the top of a camera.

"Will you PLEASE give me some space!" she yelled out, as loudly as possible. "Everybody! Please! I have an announcement to make, but you must step away and give me some space!"

As the camera pulled back she could see Chris from *The Journal* standing by with his notebook and pen, hemmed in by a number of agog faces she recognized as her neighbours. Off to one side of her front garden there was a group of six people dressed in long silver robes. They were doing a little dance and waving fluorescent glow-sticks and chanting. "What on *earth*?" gasped Aunt Thea.

"Oh, they just turned up a few minutes ago," said Chris from *The Journal*. "They're from EXTWOB."

"EXTWOB?"

"Extra Terrestrial Welcoming Organization of Britain." Chris grinned. "A bunch of loonies. They were just up the road at Stonehenge and got wind of your strange light. They think it's an alien beacon."

One of the EXTWOB dancers shimmied up towards Aunt Thea in a waft of incense, holding out a glow-stick. "We wish to help you with this great honour," she said, shaking back her purple hair and staring up into the sky. "We are here to welcome the extraterrestrial

 113

beings. We seek our sacred destiny. We seek our purpose."

"I'll give you a purpose," muttered Aunt Thea. "To stop clodhopping about on my Alpine rockery, you basket case, or it'll be your destiny to get a glow-stick up your nose."

"We do not expect to be understood," sighed the EXTWOB representative, biting sadly on her lip stud before floating back to her dance troupe. One of them had a large sign on a pole, reading: ALIENS – WE LOVE YOU!

A young, slim, fair-haired woman stepped forward holding out a microphone. "Miss Casterbridge?" She smiled sweetly. "You have something to tell us?" As the camera light got brighter again and the *Journal* photographer ran up the path, adjusting his lens, Aunt Thea took a deep breath, opened her mouth, and wondered what on earth was about to come out of it. . .

Chapter Thirteen

Oooooh – the Hoaxy Coaxy

Jack and Lewis crawled along the grass on their bellies, dragging a bin bag with them, which was filled with three torches, some heavy duty parcel tape, two mirrors and a roll of shiny blue wrapping paper. As they reached the top end of the lawn, they twisted round and stared up at the back bedroom where Sarah leaned out from the window, making a thumbs-up gesture. It looked like the photographer, and the rest of the nosy neighbours, had run round to the front to listen to Aunt Thea.

"OK, run for it!" whispered Jack, and they both got up and ran, bent over to keep as low as possible, and reached the far side of the standing stone a few seconds later. Jack crouched down,

115

with a sigh of relief. They couldn't be seen from any angle here. Even if there was a TV news helicopter above them, the overhanging branches of an elder tree shielded this side of the stone. Lewis emptied the bin bag and they began to quickly construct an "experiment" using three large torches, two mirrors and the blue paper. They taped the construction together, shining the torches upwards at an angle, towards the top of the stone.

"She's never going to believe this!" muttered Jack. "It just looks stupid!" The pale light from the three torches was nothing compared to the blue beam. "I suppose it might work from a distance." Jack bit his lip. This was not good. Not good at all.

But Lewis was pulling some paper and a pencil out of his pocket and there was a bottle of Merrion's Mead on the grass in front of him.

"What are you doing?" hissed Jack.

"Well, it's obvious, isn't it?" said Lewis. "We need Slashermite back up. I know he's busy with the register and all that but we need him now to hypnotize Sarah's cousin and *make* her believe it. Then she can go and tell them all that it's just a joke – and really believe that it *is*." He scribbled on the picture of Slashermite and spilled the mead.

"We didn't ask Aunt Thea," said Jack, doubtfully.

"We don't need to! She'll agree with us!"

"I hope you're right," said Jack.

"Ladies and gentlemen of the press and public – and er – EFTWOB," said Aunt Thea.

"EXTWOB," corrected the purple-haired glow-stick waver, swaying about behind the *Journal* photographer.

"EXTWOB then," agreed Aunt Thea with a sigh. "All of you. I have an announcement to make." She paused, wondering how far Jack and Lewis had got with their "experiment" construction. She mustn't go too fast.

"Since the dawn of time, we have looked to the stars." She waved her hand up to the sky with what she hoped was a mystical sort of look on her face. "And wondered . . . is there anything out there?"

117

The EXTWOB dancers gave a cheer and a couple of whoops.

"What strange and wonderful mysteries might await us beyond our own planet?" went on Aunt Thea. "Who can know how many other life forms may be looking down upon us? Yes, my friends, yes! This ... is something I have often wondered about." She gazed around at them all quite meaningfully, given that what she was saying was really quite meaning*less*. She checked her watch. How much longer could she spin this out?

"Tell us about the light from your garden, Miss Casterbridge," prompted Laura Trant, ruining Aunt Thea's plans to start working her way through all the alien films she could think of as good examples of interesting ideas and whatnot.

"Oh, the light," sighed the interviewee. "The ... *Light*. Well. You see, my nephews share my fascination for all things alien. We have often wondered about the crop circles in the fields around our county. Obviously, this county is the crop circle capital of the

118

world. So, anyway, we did wonder whether we could tempt an alien down here with a bit of a beacon." She saw Mrs Peebles nod her head and purse her lips, as if she'd known this all along. "So we set up some torches and so on . . . and thought we'd just . . . wait and see."

"Are you telling us your plan *worked*?" asked Laura. "That the sightings reported in the last twenty-four hours have been because of your light beam?"

"Well . . . er . . . yes and no," said Aunt Thea.

"What do you mean?"

"Well, the sightings aren't really real, you know. They're . . . well. . ."

"I tell you – I saw aliens in my garden!" shouted out Gracie Lewis from behind the cameraman. "I saw them!"

"Yes, but . . . well, that was a – a hoax!" improvised Aunt Thea, with another anxious glance at her watch. Surely Jack and Lewis would have finished their experiment building now.

"A hoax?" repeated the reporter from *The Journal*. "How was that done, then, eh?"

"Well . . . I can't explain the dragon sighting, although I think it was probably just a goose out flying through the storm," said Aunt Thea. "But the little green and blue men were . . . um . . . my nephews. Dressed up."

There were gasps of shock and murmurs of disbelief among the crowd.

"Are you saying you deliberately set this up to fool people?" asked Laura, raising one eyebrow and looking distinctly unimpressed.

"Well . . . not to fool people as such. I mean . . . that wasn't the point of the experiment. It was more about proving that people can easily be – er – mistaken. I mean, let's all be sensible, shall we? Aliens and dragons and monsters – they *don't exist*."

Aunt Thea

coughed and felt rather uncomfortable. Her neighbours – and certainly the EXTWOB people – didn't like to be taken for fools. There was angry muttering.

"Show us then!" shouted someone. "If that beam of light's just a kid's experiment, you show us!"

"I will not have the entire neighbourhood stomping through my garden," said Aunt Thea with a firm lift of her chin. "But, I will allow *you*," she pointed to the BBC reporter, "and you alone, to come in as a representative of the press."

"Aw, come *on*!" complained the *Journal* reporter, "I was here first!" But Aunt Thea was already opening the door behind her and allowing Laura in. "No! No camera!" she added, as the cameraman made to follow. Laura waved him back and followed Aunt Thea into the house.

Sarah had joined Jack and Lewis at the standing stone and was staring at Slashermite as her cousin walked up the garden with Aunt Thea. Slashermite was waiting impatiently at

121

the top of the steps that led out of the back of the stone, unseen by the approaching reporter.

"We *have* met before, haven't we?" Sarah asked him.

"Yes, Miss Sarah, we have," confirmed Slashermite.

"It's all coming back to me now," said Sarah. "I just don't know why I forgot!"

"Shhh," said Jack. "Here she comes."

Sarah turned and ran down the garden to meet Laura, who was most surprised to see her. "I'm Jack and Lewis's friend," explained Sarah, leading her cousin along by the hand.

"Don't tell me *you've* been pretending to be an alien too," said Laura.

"What me? No! I just came over for tea. And then I heard all about their experiment. Here it is."

Laura stopped a few feet away from the standing stone and gazed at the collection of mirrors, torches, blue wrapping paper and sticky tape. The three torches had been angled so that their beams met and shone on up to the stone. Her eyes followed the beam to the top of

the stone, where the *real* beam began, and she raised an eyebrow again.

She turned to Aunt Thea. "That was a good speech you made out there," she said. "You nearly had me convinced. But, look, whatever's making that light, it's not those piddly torches, is it? I'm not buying into aliens either, mind you – but a kid's experiment? I don't think so."

"That's not a problem," said Lewis. "We can convince you."

Lewis led Slashermite out from the back of the standing stone.

Laura fell into the flowerbed.

Chapter Fourteen

Fib to Camera

"Oh . . . my . . . giddy . . . aunt," gasped Laura, putting her head between her knees and then bringing it up again to stare once more at Slashermite, who was bouncing up and down a few feet in front of her, wearing his most charming smile. Laura blinked and screwed up her face in disbelief – and then stared and stared. "This . . . this could be the story of my career! It's an alien. A real live alien. Isn't it? I mean . . . that's not some kid dressed up, is it? It's . . . real. . ."

"His name is Slashermite, and he's not an alien at all. He lives on earth . . . well, *under* earth to be precise," said Aunt Thea. "We'd love to tell you the whole story, but I really

don't think we have time."

Jack spotted the *Journal* photographer at the bathroom window of next door's house again. They had placed Slashermite in a position where he was shielded from the camera lens by the standing stone, and made sure he didn't move out into view.

"But you're welcome to get a closer look at him," went on Aunt Thea, as Laura raised her head to stare at the Mite again. "He's quite safe. Lewis, take Laura across to meet Slashermite."

"You said," whispered Laura, pulling a twig out of her hair, "that there were no such things as dragons or monsters or aliens. . ."

"Yes, well . . . I lied," admitted Aunt Thea.

Lewis took Laura's trembling hand and led her across to Slashermite, where she sank to her knees in front of him and stared, open mouthed, at all his purple, spiky, finger-bladey weirdness. Then Lewis whispered in Slashermite's ear and at once the Mite began to waft his finger-blades back and forth in a mesmerizing way. Laura gasped and edged back a little.

 125

"It's fine – he won't hurt you. He's very nice, really," said Aunt Thea. "Just look at him!"

Laura's eyes grew large and dark as she stared at the creature and his mesmerizing hands.

Slashermite opened his mouth and said, in a dreamy, slow voice: "You will only remember—"

And then he flipped over backwards.

"NO!" shouted Sarah, as she sent Slashermite sprawling across the grass in great surprise. "Oh no you *don't*!"

"You what?" spluttered Jack, while Lewis shouted, "Oy! Don't shove my Mite!"

"That's what you did to me, wasn't it? You got Slashermite to hypnotize me to forget! I remember now!" Sarah looked outraged.

Jack, Lewis and Aunt Thea glanced around at each other, uncomfortably.

"And you were just going to do the same thing again to Laura! Well, I won't let you! Honestly! I help you and then you zap my brain! Thanks a bunch! And now you want Laura's help and you're going to zap *her* brain.

126

It's just not on!"

"It was only for the safety of the planet," mumbled Jack, guiltily.

Laura was gaping around at them all. "What on earth is going on?"

"Right, change of plan!" sighed Aunt Thea. "Laura, we need your help. We have to get rid of the press and the neighbours and the loonies with the glow-sticks. In return, we will tell you the most extraordinary story of your career."

Laura was shaking her head in wonder. "More extraordinary than – *that?*" She pointed at Slashermite, who was getting to his feet, looking quite put out.

"You have *no idea*," said Aunt Thea. "But first, how can we get rid of the crowd out front?"

"Have you tried switching that off?" Laura pointed up to the light.

Aunt Thea clicked her teeth. "To quote my nephews – 'well . . . dur!'. Of course we have. Nothing works."

"OK, then . . . we have to come up with something even more exciting . . . somewhere

 127

else," said Laura. "A long way from here. So this is boring in comparison."

"Great, well, can't you run out and tell them there's a big story – up north of the county, or something?"

Laura narrowed her eyes. "Look, I report on stories. I don't make them up."

"No need!" said Jack, suddenly. "Come on. Everyone back to the kitchen. We've got work to do . . . and fast!"

"Wait, Slashermite, sorry, you have to go back down again," said Lewis. His Mite looked rather cheesed off. "Sorry to keep sending you up and down, but you'll get seen if we go down the garden. Oh – and did you do the register?"

"Yes, Master Lewis," said Slashermite. "Here it is." And he handed Lewis a rolled piece of parchment paper with a long list of names on it. "And I have to tell you. . ."

"Not now, Slashy – go back home, OK?" Lewis shoved the parchment in his pocket and waved his creation off as he ran to join the others in the kitchen. He didn't notice how his

 128

Mite stood for a few seconds, anxiously scraping his finger-blades together, before shaking his purple head and going back through the Gateway to Tauronia.

Jack was at the table with the paper and the crayons and the Merrion's Mead. As he worked on his drawing, Aunt Thea sat Laura down and did her best to explain all about the mead and the monsters and Tauronia. Sarah added bits from time to time and kept nodding and laughing, "It's true! It's all true!"

"So," said Laura. "Will you let me see Tauronia? When I've helped you get rid of the crowd?" They could still hear everyone murmuring, chanting and talking on mobile phones outside the front door.

"Not on your life!" shuddered Aunt Thea. "Nobody goes to Tauronia! It's unspeakably dangerous." Laura looked sceptical, so she added. "It was created by a seven-year-old and a nine-year-old! Boys!"

Laura pursed her lips, thought for a bit and then said, "Ah."

129

"But I suppose we could bring a few of its inhabitants up to meet you," said Aunt Thea. "Electrotaur and Slashermite and maybe Blomonjataur and the Jellymites. . . They should be fairly safe."

Jack finished his drawing, and held it up. "Well," he said. "What do you think? Will this create a distraction?"

On the paper, in violet and blue crayon, floated SPACEMITE. He was a weird, blobby, saucer-shaped thing, with lots of floating tentacles, many yellow eyes around his domed head and short purple aerials sticking out of him at intervals. He looked a bit like a spinning, grinning jellyfish.

"We need to put him in the sky – somewhere miles away from here," said Jack. "So everyone can see

130

him and all the alien hunters will leave us and go to find Spacemite."

"Jack, that's brilliant," said Aunt Thea, clapping him on the head. "Now, where shall we send him?"

"Umm," Jack frowned. "I don't know."

"Over Stonehenge?" suggested Sarah. "People are always up there looking for aliens. Or over a field where there's been a crop circle or something."

Aunt Thea suddenly stood up straight. "I know just the place," she said. "Jack, can you send it to a farm just north of Avebury?"

"Um, I don't know," said Jack. "Have I been there?"

"Well, no," said Aunt Thea. "Why?"

"Because I have to have *seen* it to know where to send Spacemite," said Jack. "It has to be somewhere in my head, not just on a map. Or I can't dream it and draw Spacemite into the right place. He could show up just anywhere otherwise."

Aunt Thea bit her lip. "Hmm . . . right . . . in that case we have to drive there and deliver

 131

Spacemite into the sky ourselves. OK, let's go."

"Er, haven't you forgotten something?" said Laura.

"Ah yes," said Aunt Thea. "Right. Now. This is where you come in. . ."

The blinding light of two TV cameras flared into Laura's face as she opened the door. More press had arrived. The local ITV news crew had now pitched up. She gulped. She was very nervous. She was about to say something – on camera (her own and ITV's!) – which she knew wasn't true. And then something off camera which was even less true. So far.

And she was trusting her reputation to a nine-year-old boy's *drawing*!

What if it didn't work? What if this *was* all an elaborate hoax? Maybe that thing *was* a kid dressed up to look like an alien? But then, she reflected, Sarah wouldn't do that to her cousin. Would she? Maybe she'd forgotten her last birthday or something, though.

"Laura Trant! What's going on in there?" demanded the reporter from ITV, poking a

 132

microphone into her face.

Laura sighed and shook her head with a rueful smile. "It's a hoax, people! Don't waste your time. It was an experiment with some theatrical lighting – they've been betting on how much press attention they can stir up. And they've done really well." She winked at the ITV camera.

Then she leaned forward and grabbed the arm of her own cameraman. "Come on, Bob," she muttered, quietly – but just loud enough for the ITV crew to hear. "I know where a *real* story is. We've got to get there fast!"

"You what?" said Bob, switching off his camera and peering at her. Laura pulled him over to the hedge and said, "Ryedale Farm – just north of Avebury Ring. There's a real UFO sighting going on there – RIGHT NOW!" She waved her mobile phone at him and pretended not to notice the ITV reporter sidling up and listening in. "That's *Ryedale Farm*! Newsdesk just rang through and told us to get there on the double!"

133

The ITV crew suddenly dashed for their van and Laura ran for the BBC truck, Bob trailing after her, carrying his heavy gear. Once in the van, with his gear stashed behind the front seats, Bob reached for the ignition key and brummed the engine.

"Wait!" said Laura. "Switch it off!"

"Make your mind up, love!" said Bob. "You said at the double!"

"Yes, I know. But you have to make it seem like the engine won't start."

"Are you nuts? The ITV crew have already gone! You could have kept your voice down! The *Journal* guys are going after them too. Even the bloomin' neighbours!"

Outside, several excited neighbours jumped into a couple of cars and raced off after the press, shouting, "UFO sighting! There's a UFO up near Avebury! Right now!" Mrs Peebles was driving like a demon. They'd never had such a good time. Just behind them, all the EXTWOB people were urgently wafting into a VW Camper van.

"Trust me!" said Laura and Bob shook his

134

head, sighed, and made the engine cough a few times, to make it look as if they'd broken down.

When everyone else had gone, the front door of Aunt Thea's cottage opened and out trotted Jack, Lewis, Sarah and Aunt Thea. Jack had a drawing pad, some crayons and a little knobbly wooden bottle in his hands. They walked sedately to the BBC van and then got in behind Laura and Bob. There wasn't much space as it was filled with broadcasting equipment. The seats behind were really just boxes on the floor of the vehicle. But there was just enough room.

"Right, so I guess we're *not* going to Ryedale Farm, just north of Avebury," said Bob, with a grin.

"Actually we *are* going there," said Aunt Thea.

"But everyone else will have got the story before we get there!" wailed Bob, hurriedly getting the engine going again.

"Trust us," said Jack. "There won't be a story *until* we get there."

135

Aunt Thea was on her mobile phone. "Carol!" she called down it. "It's Thea. Now listen to me, carefully! You're going to get a film crew and a load of press and other mad people showing up in the next fifteen minutes. Now, whatever they say to you, agree that it's true. Just keep nodding – and let them on to your top field to film whatever they want to film. I will be there in twenty minutes and will explain everything. Yes! No – I'm not insane. Well, only slightly. Don't worry. This is very good news!"

The van sped along as the evening grew darker, taking corners fast so that the passengers in the back had to grab hold of straps and rails. Jack tucked the bottle of mead into his T-shirt pocket, looked down at his picture of Spacemite and grinned. He was going to enjoy watching him appear up in the sky above the farm.

Then Bob went over a speed bump at forty mph. Everyone thwacked up and down in their seats and the bottle of mead shot up out of Jack's pocket, spun once in the air and smacked down on to the drawing. Its cork

136

was knocked out and mead spilled across Spacemite's face.

Before Jack could even shout *NO!* the air around them went *Ker-pow!* and they were suddenly squashed sideways by the arrival, in the BBC satellite van, of a large alien monster.

Chapter Fifteen

A Little More Spacemite Be Nice?

"AAAAAAAAARRRRRRRGGGGHHHH," commented Bob, from the driver's seat. Fortunately Spacemite was mostly billowing his semi-see-through bulgy body about in the *back* of the truck. Although Laura and Bob were shoved forward in their seats, they hadn't, thankfully, been knocked right through the windscreen. Bob was still able to drive, but a backward glance had made him shriek with terror. Understandably. There was a rather large alien leaning on his shoulder.

"What'ff going ffON?" shrieked Aunt Thea, her face full of Spacemite.

"Fff meadff! It fflew wout offfffmy fpwocket!" explained Jack, as well as he was able to.

138

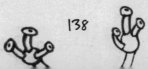

Spacemite's jellyfish-like body, all blue and violet bulges and bright yellow eyes, was squished tightly into the back of the truck, pinning them all against the sides or bits of broadcasting equipment. It was hard to find enough space even to breathe.

"FfLewishh! Ffplarah! Pwah!" Aunt Thea managed to get her hand up and push a bit of Spacemite away from her face. "Lewis! Sarah! Are you both OK?"

"Mmmawright!" called back Lewis, raising a thumb above a coil of glowing tentacles.

"Me too," yelled Sarah. She had her head in a gap in some metal shelving and was holding the surge of Spacemite back with both hands.

Jack had also managed to push the alien blubber away from his face now. "The mead burst open on the picture when we went over that bump!" he said, in a strained voice. "So Spacemite just came to life – here! I hadn't drawn him into any particular place yet, so he just showed up in the place I was looking at, at the time."

139

"Well, get rid of him!" demanded Aunt Thea. "We're going to choke!"

"I can't! There's no way I can reach the picture or the mead or the crayons," wailed Jack. "I can't *move!*"

"Well, this is just fantastic," sighed Laura at the front. "I'm off to a UFO sighting only to find the UFO is IN MY HAIR!"

"Oh, why did you have to make him so big?" moaned Aunt Thea, pushing something dribbly and curly out of her ear. "Mites are supposed to be *small!*"

"Well, he was meant to be seen from miles around!" squawked Jack. "He had to be big. In fact he's much bigger than *this!* He's all squished up at the moment. He'll be three times this size when he gets out. When I get round to drawing Space*taur,* that one will be immense. And then Spacemite will seem quite small."

"Jnack. . ." came Lewis's rather muffled voice, aggrieved, offended and slightly panicky. "He'th justh sthtuck something up by thnose!"

140

"SPACEMITE!" Jack gave the creature a prod with his knuckles. "Stop probing at once! You're not allowed to probe any people! Do you hear me? Get out of Lewis's nose immediately!"

There was a sticky, slurping sound and then Lewis called out. "OK, he's taken half my brain out, but he's stopped probing."

"Sorry, Lew," sighed Jack. "But it's what aliens do, isn't it? They probe. For experiments and that."

"Sorry to break in on all this nose-picking fun with ET!" snapped Laura. "But what the heck are we meant to do now? I'm *not* driving up to a crowd of press, who *all know* me, by the way, and sliding out with an alien stuck in my hair! It'll be all over the news! All over the internet in seconds! I will never have a life of my own ever again! Nor will the rest of you. We have to sort this out – NOW!"

"OK, calm down! Now . . . don't go all the way to Ryedale Farm, Bob," said Aunt Thea. "There's a little wood off the road, a mile or so before you get there. Let's pull in there and

 141

release Spacemite into the sky where nobody can see us."

"Good idea," said Laura. "All right, Bob?"

Bob, still driving with his head pressed against the windscreen, managed to give her a *look*. "I'm never coming out on a job with you again," he promised.

It was a wonder they weren't stopped by the police, thought Lewis, as they pelted at top speed through the country lanes. Bob was desperate to get the alien off the back of his neck, and so they arrived at the little wood in just five minutes. Laura scrambled out of the front passenger door and then ran around and slid back the truck's side door. There was an icky, slithery, gloopy noise and everyone came out of the truck, stuck to Spacemite, in an avalanche of extraterrestrial goo.

"Yuck!" shuddered Sarah. "There's alien squish all over me!"

The truck had stopped in a little clearing among the trees, and as Aunt Thea, Jack, Lewis and Sarah peeled themselves off Spacemite with little plops and squelches,

the creature suddenly bloomed out and up, like a balloon being filled with gas. It was indeed, huge. And now it floated gently off the ground, just above their heads, and its curly, stringy, pale violet tentacles draped over their heads. Its many yellow eyes blinked one after the other like Christmas tree lights set to "twinkle".

"He's actually quite pretty – at a distance," said Aunt Thea with a forgiving smile. "And he's going to do wonderful things for Ryedale Farm. Now, Jack, look down there through the trees. You see those buildings? They are the barns at the top field of Carol's farm."

Everyone peered in the direction of Aunt Thea's outstretched finger. The farm buildings were nestled into the gently rolling fields. One straight farm track ran along the top end towards the barns. They could see headlights of several vehicles dashing along it.

"Drat and blast!" huffed Bob. "They've all beaten us to it! ITV's going to get the UFO shots before we do!"

Laura patted his head. "Bob, the UFO is here, with *us*! We're just going to send it into the night sky so they can see it!" She looked around at them all. "I think he's slightly concussed," she explained.

"Right, Jack, concentrate," went on Aunt Thea. "You need to send Spacemite into the skies above the farm – and he must be there for a little while – about ten minutes. Long enough for them to get lots of good stuff on film, but not long enough for the Ministry of Defence to send military jets, OK?"

"Yep," said Jack. "Just the one show? And then he goes back to Tauronia?"

"No, wait," said Aunt Thea, looking thoughtful. "He needs to pop back from time to time. Nine or ten times a year, I would say. Randomly. Whenever he fancies it. Or whenever we ask him to. And when he's had a bit of a play in the sky, he must blink out of sight and then go straight back to Tauronia and hang around in the Tauronian sky instead. But first, our sky. Obviously, he can't land at any point."

Jack turned his head up to his creature, which was now the size of a small circus tent. "You do look fantastic!" he said proudly. Then he related everything that he and Aunt Thea had agreed. "You're doing a good job for us here, Spacemite," he finished. Spacemite held out a tentacle and Jack shook it. "Off you go then!" he said and they all stood back.

145

Spacemite suddenly shot up through the gap in the trees. He glowed fantastically and made straight for the sky above the barns, swooping and darting and leaving a fading trail of luminous violet behind him. His many eyes sparkled with golden light and another shiny part of him went round and round like a spinning saucer. Down by the barn, little camera flashes could be seen.

"Wow!" said Lewis. "He looks brilliant! That's one of the best you've ever created, Jack!"

"We should get down there now," said Bob, looking dazed. "Get the shots! Newsdesk will go mad! They said we had to get there on the double."

They all got back into the van and by the time they reached the barns a few minutes later, the press and TV people were shrieking and whooping with excitement. The members of EXTWOB had formed a circle and were lying flat on their backs in the soggy wheatfield, waving their legs and arms in the air and singing.

146

Carol and her husband were standing alongside them, staring up, open mouthed as Spacemite looped the loop among the stars.

Aunt Thea went up to them. "Did you say what I said to say?" she asked Carol. Carol just gaped at her.

"OK, now, remember. Here is your story. You've seen this a few times, but you thought it was just a weather balloon. It shows up time and again. Only over this field."

Carol nodded.

"Lots of people are going to want to come and camp here," said Aunt Thea. "They will want to spend time looking for aliens. They will probably need feeding. Toilet facilities. Maybe a café and gift shop at some stage. But for now, you can just start charging people, after tonight, for camping on your land. You're going to make a lot of money out of this field. Enough to keep your farm and carry on using all the other fields as usual. Like your family has done for centuries. OK?"

 147

"Do you think she understood any of that?" asked Laura as Aunt Thea wandered back towards the BBC truck.

"Maybe not right now," said Aunt Thea. "There *is* a UFO up there, after all. But she'll work it all out tomorrow. I will phone her again."

"Woo hoo!" shouted Sarah and Lewis and Jack, as they watched the fantastic display from a little way up the hill, well away from the crowd. And then "Ooo-er!" as Spacemite swooped down behind a hedge and then bobbed up again with a very panicked farm cat in his tentacles.

"Spacemite! Put it down! No probing!" shouted Jack. Spacemite dropped the cat, reluctantly, and whizzed up into the air again. The cat retched up a furball and ran for its life. Fortunately, the cameras wouldn't have seen what *they* had seen on the other side of the hedge. Jack hastily scribbled, *No coming below 100 feet above ground!* alongside his drawing and quickly meaded it with what was left in the bottle.

Four minutes later Spacemite did a corkscrew swoop over the film crews and photographers and then shot up into space before blinking out of sight.

The BBC crew packed up and went. Nobody else noticed. They would be camped out there for some time yet, hoping for more. But Laura knew there wouldn't be another sighting for a few weeks now.

"Well, you were brilliant, Laura – and you too, Bob," said Aunt Thea, as they drove back. "Nobody's going to waste any more time on reporting some piddly little blue light from my back garden now. Not with a proper UFO sighting going on here!"

"But we've still got to find a way to stop that light," said Jack. "Or eventually they're going to come back. Your neighbours are going to keep asking about it, aren't they?"

"There must be something you can put on it," said Laura. "To stop the light coming through! How about metal? A big bin lid or something?"

"Something on it," Aunt Thea was muttering.

"Put something *on* it. . ." She sat up, suddenly, on the box in the back of the van. "Jack! Lewis! Remember when we cleaned the stone last week? You used up all my lavender oil, didn't you?"

"Nearly all," said Jack. "There was a tiny bit left in that third bottle when we'd finished."

"But Jack, I didn't *have* a third bottle! I only had two."

"But. . ." Jack wrinkled his brow. "There was another bottle – a little plastic one, just like the other two."

"And did it smell the same?" Aunt Thea leaned forward and stared at Jack and then at Lewis. "Did it?"

"I don't know!" squeaked Jack. "There was so much lavender smell up my nose I couldn't tell what a bacon sandwich smelled like! It was a bit runny though . . . runnier than the other stuff."

Aunt Thea grinned. "Jack, you dingbat! You didn't use lavender oil on it. You used Merrion's Mead!"

Jack gaped at her and then babbled, "What . . . how . . . where?"

"It was the mead that got stolen! And when we got it back, it was in a little plastic bottle – which looked just like my lavender oil bottles. We must have forgotten to empty it back into a proper wooden bottle. Obviously it got mixed up with my lavender oils."

"So, we *meaded* the stone without even knowing it?" cried Lewis. "And just as I was saying how much it looked like a beacon to attract aliens! But I didn't *draw* it, did I?"

"No," said Jack. "But maybe we don't have to. As long as we dream it, the mead makes it come true."

"So all you need to do is mead it again and undo your dream, Lewis," sighed Aunt Thea. "Thank goodness all this madness is over!"

Chapter Sixteen

A Bolt for the Blue

"You'd better *both* mead it, to be sure," said Aunt Thea, anxiously eyeing the drawing of the standing stone that both Jack and Lewis had just made. Alongside it Lewis had crayoned the words "NOT an alien beacon". The brothers stood beside the actual stone and each dropped a little mead on to the paper before staring up hopefully.

"Is this what they use to bring the monsters to life – this mead stuff?" Laura asked Sarah, who nodded and grinned. She couldn't wait for her cousin to see some of the Taurs. Beside them stood Bob, staring at the action around the stone, looking dazed. Laura had tried to explain what Aunt Thea had explained about

Tauronia and the mead and so on – but she didn't think he was taking it in.

"Oh, it's no *good*!" wailed Lewis after a few seconds. "It's still there! And the neighbours will be back any time now. They'll have got bored waiting for another Spacemite show."

"We must be missing something!" said Jack. "What?"

"Maybe you need to mead the stone itself again," suggested Aunt Thea.

Both Jack and Lewis rubbed more mead on the stone – but after several minutes nothing had changed and Aunt Thea was beginning to look desperate.

"I know!" said Lewis. "The lightning! It was the lightning!"

"Are you saying we need *another* lightning strike?" said Aunt Thea, getting up again and pressing a hand to the stone.

"Yes! That's the only thing we haven't tried! That must be how the light got switched on, and that's what will turn it off again!"

"Oh great." Aunt Thea rubbed her brow. "So now we have to start messing with the laws

 153

of nature. Oh, this is *so* not good. I'm not sure even Merrion's Mead can make that happen – and I'm very definitely not sure that I should allow it."

"You don't need to," said Jack. "All we need is Electrotaur."

Aunt Thea made Laura and Bob sit down. "Stay with them, Sarah," she urged. "You've seen Electrotaur and you know he can be a little scary."

From the far side of the stone a golden glow suddenly shafted across the dark bushes. Then Slashermite scampered around to greet their guests, with a wary look at Sarah.

"What the. . ." squawked Bob and Laura took a deep breath and gazed in wonder once again.

"AAAAAARRRRRRGH!" added Bob as Electrotaur stepped majestically into view.

"I ASSIST," rumbled the eight foot tall monster, as little sparks of light streamed from his finger and tail tips and danced within his green eyes. You would have to know him well

154

to see it, as Electrotaur wasn't the emotional type, but Jack could tell he was excited. He had a quest and there is nothing that Taurs like more than a quest.

Laura and Bob clung to each other, whimpering, and Sarah patted their shoulders and whispered, "It's OK, he won't hurt you. Probably."

"Electrotaur, please send a bolt of lightning into the top of the standing stone," commanded Jack. "But not a little one – this has to be a HUGE bolt of lightning. You really have to give it everything you've got. Here –" he leaned across and turned the purple dial on Electrotaur's chest right up to full power. The Taur began to shake and buzz like an overheating boiler. "You might want to get back a bit," advised Jack, grabbing Lewis's arm and pulling him away from the stone.

Electrotaur gazed across at the top of the standing stone. His eyes were like green fire and shower after shower of sparks flew from his fingers, tail and even his toes. Now he raised one lightning-fingered hand and the air around

 155

them seemed to hum with captive electricity. There was a hot metal smell pulsing through it, and everyone's hair began to stand out on end. They looked like a bunch of dandelion clocks.

Then KAPOWZZZZZZZICRAKKKKKK!!!

The noise and the power took everyone's breath away. The light was so blindingly white that Lewis was certain he could *feel* his eyeballs shrinking. Then a second later it was all over and Electrotaur was sagging forward like a broken doll, two tiny green dots showing in the dark pools of his eyes. He was totally out of power.

As they all blinked and tried to sort out their eyeballs, Aunt Thea gave a whoop of relief. The evening sky was navy and empty. At last, the pillar of blue light was gone.

In the kitchen they drank hot chocolate and ate shortbread while Jack and Lewis and Sarah pressed small batteries against Electrotaur's fingers until he came back on line again. His power dial was down very low. But he was awake enough now to suck on a nine-volt, and looked better. Aunt Thea made Slashermite some more porridge with pretend ants in it (currants this time).

They spent some enjoyable time telling Laura and Bob all about Tauronia and showing them the many pictures that Jack and Lewis had drawn and meaded into life. The pair were pale and shocked but Laura's eyes glimmered with excitement. "I can't believe there's a whole underground world that nobody else knows about," she sighed, shaking her head. "Let me see it! Oh please – just once. Just a peep."

"No, nobody goes down there," said Aunt Thea. "I told you – it's horrifically dangerous for humans."

"But *they've* been!" protested Laura, waving at Jack and Lewis. "They've been there getting chased by Grippakrunchataur or whatever and outrunning avalanches of custard and all that – and they're all right!"

"Only *just*!" said Jack. "We were nearly eaten! Or drowned! Or *hugged*!" He shuddered at the memory of *that* adventure.

"But, if I just have a little look from the gateway. . ."

Aunt Thea sighed and nodded at Jack and Lewis. "Come on," said Jack, to Sarah. "Help me and Lewis get Electrotaur back up the garden and through the Gateway to Tauronia.

He needs to get home and recharge his batteries." Lewis paused to whisper something in Slashermite's ear as Laura went on pleading with Aunt Thea.

"Well . . . there is *one* way you might get to see it," said Aunt Thea. "But I still think it could be really dangerous. . ."

"What? What?" Laura clapped her hands, her brown eyes sparkling with excitement.

"Well, you'll have to do a sort of – *mind meld* – with Slashermite. He will bring you into his thoughts so you can see Tauronia through his eyes. It's not the same as actually going there, but maybe if you can handle what you see, we can talk about that another time."

"OK – mind meld. Go for it," said Laura.

"Very well. Laura, and you too Bob, you need to watch Slashermite's eyes for the mind meld to begin."

They stared at Slashermite's bright glittery eyes, and didn't really notice when his finger-blades started doing their little dance.

 159

Chapter Seventeen

Waving Goodbye

"Where are Laura and Bob?" asked Sarah as they all burst back into the kitchen.

"Gone back to the BBC," said Aunt Thea. "Newsroom called. They had to rush off and get their alien sighting on tonight's late bulletin, before ITV beat them to it."

Slashermite examined his finger-blades intently and whistled a little tune. He and Aunt Thea did not mention that Laura and Bob had gone happily back to work with absolutely no memory of anything called a Taur or a Mite or a mad underground world called Tauronia.

"My mum will be here to collect me soon, too," sighed Sarah. "I've had a brilliant day!

I can't believe we chased down Flowertaur, brought Baz back from the dead and launched our own alien into space! Will we get to see Spacemite again?"

"Sure to," said Aunt Thea. "He's scheduled for another visit next month. I just had a phone call from Carol. EXTWOB have asked to rent her spare barn for their new headquarters. They're going to pay her enough to sort out all her money problems. Of course, she'll have to deal with the glow-sticks and the singing and dancing. . . but there's talk of a visitor centre and gift shop already. So it's all turned out very well. And for us too! No more alien beacon – no more sightings! No more flowery assassins roaming the local parks. Come and sit down on the sofa, all of you, and relax for a while before Sarah's mum comes."

They all slumped down on Aunt Thea's comfy sofa, exhausted. They could just make out the noise of the neighbours arriving back, all chattering with excitement over the alien sighting. Nobody knocked on the door to ask what had happened to the blue light.

Slashermite sat down on a leather pouffe near Sarah and started waving at her. She waved back. "Hi, Slashy – sorry about pushing you over earlier."

"That's quite all right, Miss Sarah," he grinned, toothily, still waving. Sarah grinned back.

162

"It was only because I didn't want to . . . um . . . what was it I didn't want?" Sarah frowned and rubbed her nose, still staring at Slashermite.

"You didn't want to worry about anything," said Slashermite. Sarah hadn't noticed when Lewis got up to whisper in his ear. She couldn't even see Lewis.

"You wanted to have a little sleep and then wake up with nothing in your head at all to do with Tauronia."

"Yes . . . that was it. . ." Sarah smiled sleepily and then conked out on Aunt Thea's best beaded cushion.

Chapter Eighteen

Bang On, Mum

"So, is it a hoax, or is it real? We've talked to experts and they say they just can't tell!" concluded the morning news presenter. "For now, we'll just have to go on wondering whether the Jellyfish Alien, as he's already been dubbed, will come again. . ."

"He's not called the Jellyfish Alien!" spluttered Lewis, through a mouthful of Shreddies. "He's called Spacemite!"

"Really, Lewis," chuckled Mum, pouring herself some coffee. "You act as if you've *met* the alien!"

"I have," huffed Lewis. "He stuck a tentacle up my nose and probed my brain."

Jack frowned at his brother, but Lewis just shrugged. They knew Mum never believed a

164

word of it anyway.

"You know, I sometimes wonder," she said, standing at the kitchen window and looking out into the garden, "whether there really are unexplained things out there. I mean, take all these little green or blue men sightings. I could have *sworn* that I just saw a little navy blue creature with a bandage thing over his face leaping through the trees at the end of the garden – and then just vanishing."

Jack choked on his milk and Lewis suddenly lurched in his seat and went into spasms of searching through all his pockets.

"Probably just too much caffeine," laughed Mum, turning away from the window and collecting her toast as it popped up. As she opened the jam jar, Lewis found what he was looking for. Slashermite's register of Taurs and Mites. With shaking hands Lewis unrolled the paper to reveal a very long list of names, written in Slashermite's spidery script, under the title: PRESENT & CORRECT IN TAURONIA.

Then, at the bottom, there was a new title – MISSING.

Below it was just one name.

Ninjataur.

Lewis flew up the back garden and saw a blue silk clad foot swinging down from the plum tree behind the shed. He stopped under the tree, panting, and tried to steady his voice. "Ninjataur. You are not meant to be out! You should have gone back down to Tauronia with the others."

Ninjataur stared down at his creator, silver eyes glittering through a slit in his blue silk mask. He stretched lazily and looked around him, as if planning to go. Lewis stood tall and said, commandingly: "I am your creator and I demand that you stay still."

To his surprise and relief, Ninjataur's stretching and leg swinging abruptly stopped. Jack arrived, also panting, with the paper, a pencil and the mead. Lewis was mightily relieved that Jack had come home with the bottle still in his pocket after last night's adventures. They'd have to deliver it back to Aunt Thea, of course, but it was very good luck that they had it now.

He quickly drew Ninjataur and wrote "Returns to Tauronia immedietly" alongside the sketch, but paused before allowing Jack to mead it. "Are you sure he can't just stay a little while and play?" He eyed the Taur hopefully.

"Not on your life!" said Jack. "Mum's coming up the garden!" He splonshed on the last of the mead.

"What are you two up to?" said Mum, a few

feet behind them. Jack and Lewis stared at their mum and then back at Ninjataur, panic rising in their chests. "Come *on*!" whispered Jack, shaking the damp drawing urgently.

"What are you staring up at the tree for?" chuckled Mum, stepping up beside Lewis.

With a small *pop* Ninjataur disappeared – half a second before Mum looked up.

"What made you both rush up the garden?" she added.

"The creature you saw up in the tree," said Lewis. "It was one of my monsters. We had to come and catch him and get him back to Tauronia."

Mum smiled at him and ruffled his hair. "You two! You're so funny. You really believe your monsters are real, don't you?"

"They *are* real," said Lewis.

"Yes, of course they are, Lew. Of course they are." She put her arms around their shoulders and walked them back down the garden. "Just like that dragon in the storm. You'll be telling me next that you both went flying on it."

"We did," said Lewis.

"Oh! Well, *of course* you did."

"And Jack fell off and nearly died, but he was saved by landing on one of my other monsters, who's made of blancmange."

"All right, Lewis – now you're just being silly. . ."

**Look out for the other
Monster Makers adventures**

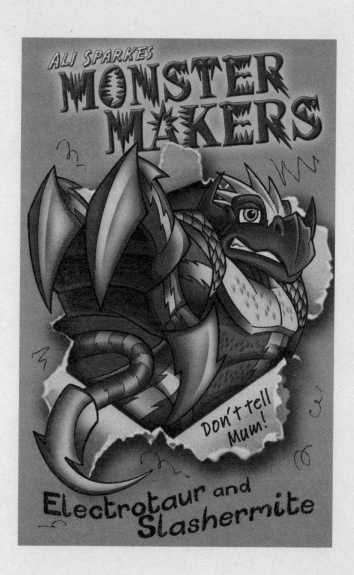